By Thornton Wilder

SAMUEL FRENCH, INC.

45 WEST 25TH STREET   NEW YORK 10010
7623 SUNSET BOULEVARD   HOLLYWOOD 90046
LONDON   *TORONTO*

THE MATCHMAKER

STORY OF THE PLAY

(9 males; 7 females)

A certain old merchant of Yonkers is now so rich that he decides to take a wife. To this end he employs a matchmaker, a woman who subsequently becomes involved with two of his menial clerks, assorted young and lovely ladies, and the headwaiter at an expensive restaurant where this swift farce runs headlong into a hilarious climax of complication. After everyone gets all straightened out romantically, and everyone has his heart's desire, the merchant of Yonkers finds himself affianced to the astute matchmaker herself. He who was so shrewd in business is putty in the hands of a player like Ruth Gordon, who played the matchmaker. He is fooled by apprentices in a series of hilarious hide-and-seek scenes, and finally has all his bluster explode in his face.

This play is a rewritten version of the play "THE MERCHANT OF YONKERS" which was directed in 1938 by Max Reinhardt and is again dedicated to

MAX REINHARDT

with deep admiration and indebtedness.

This play is based upon a comedy by Johann Nestroy, *Einen Jux will es sich Machen* (Vienna, 1842) which was in turn based upon an English original, *A Day Well Spent* (London, 1835) by John Oxenford.

THE MERCHANT OF YONKERS was produced by Herman Shumlin and directed by Max Reinhardt. The production was designed by Boris Aronson. The cast included Jane Cowl, June Walker, Nydia Westman, Minna Phillips, Percy Waram, Tom Ewell, John Call, Joseph Sweeney, Philip Coolidge, and Edward Nannery. It was first performed on December 12, 1938, at the Colonial Theatre, Boston. The New York engagement opened at the Guild Theatre on December 28, 1938.

THE MATCHMAKER was produced for the Edinburgh Festival by Tennent Productions. It was directed by Dr. Tyrone Guthrie and the production was designed by Tanya Moiseiwitsch. The first performance was at the Royal Lyceum Theatre, Edinburgh, on August 23, 1954.

The same production opened at the Theatre Royal Haymarket, London, on November 4, 1954. Without changes in the principal roles—with the exception of that of Mr. Vandergelder, which was played successively by Sam Levene, Eddie Mayhoff, and Loring Smith—the play was performed at the Locust Street Theatre, Philadelphia, on October 27, 1955.

THE MATCHMAKER

Comedy by Thornton Wilder; staged by Tyrone Guthrie; settings and costumes by Tanya Moiseiwitsch; presented by the Theatre Guild and David Merrick·at the Royale Theatre, December 5, 1955.

6

The cast:

HORACE VANDERGELDER .... *Loring Smith*
AMBROSE KEMPER .... *Alexander Davion*
JOE SCANLON .... *Philip Leeds*
GERTRUDE .... *Charity Grace*
CORNELIUS HACKL .... *Arthur Hill*
ERMENGARDE .... *Prunella Scales*
MALACHI STACK .... *Patrick McAlinney*
MRS. LEVI .... *Ruth Gordon*
BARNABY TUCKER .... *Robert Morse*
MRS. MOLLOY .... *Eileen Herlie*
MINNIE FAY .... *Rosamund Greenwood*
A CABMAN .... *Peter Bayliss*
RUDOLF .... *William Lanteau*
AUGUST .... *John Milligan*
MISS FLORA VAN HUYSEN ...... *Esme Church*
HER COOK .... *Christine Thomas*

Cast of the London production:

HORACE VANDERGELDER, *a merchant of Yonkers, N. Y.*
                                        SAM LEVENE
CORNELIUS HACKL ⎱ *Clerks*   ARTHUR HILL
BARNABY TUCKER ⎬ *in his*   ALEC McCOWEN
MALACHI STACK ⎰ *store*   PATRICK McALINNEY
AMBROSE KEMPER, *an artist*   LEE MONTAGUE
JOE SCANLON, *a barber*   PETER SALLIS
RUDOLPH ⎱ *waiters*   TIMOTHY FINDLEY
AUGUST ⎰   JOHN MILLIGAN
A CABMAN   PETER BAYLISS

MRS. DOLLY LEVI ⎱ *friends of* RUTH GORDON
MISS FLORA VAN HUYSEN ⎰ *Vandergelder's late wife* ESME CHURCH

MRS. IRENE MOLLOY, *milliner*   EILEEN HERLIE
MINNIE FAY, *her assistant*   ROSAMUND GREENWOOD
ERMENGARDE, *Vandergelder's niece*   PRUNELLA SCALES
GERTRUDE, *Vandergelder's housekeeper* HENZIE RAEBURN
MISS VAN HUYSEN'S COOK   DAPHNE NEWTON
A MUSICIAN   PETER SALLIS

SYNOPSIS OF SCENES

TIME: *The early 80's.*

ACT I
Vandergelder's house in Yonkers, N. Y.

ACT II
Mrs. Molloy's hat store, New York.

ACT III
The Harmonia Gardens Restaurant on the Battery.

ACT IV
Miss Van Huysen's house.

The sets are not "solid," but consist of cloths for the back walls and open wings for the side walls. All curtains, pelmets, drapes, etc., are painted. There is a permanent false proscenium painted bamboo trellis and roses.

The Matchmaker

ACT ONE

At the end of the overture, the house lights begin to fade, the orchestra goes into "East Side, West Side" as Curtain music, and the Act drop rises to disclose a front cloth. This cloth is painted in the theme of the journey from Yonkers to New York, with an 18th century train centre, a view of Yonkers Right and the city of New York Left. Towards the end of the thirty-two bars of music, this cloth goes away, revealing the living room of Vandergelder's house above his store, Yonkers, New York, in the early eighties. Articles from the store have overflowed into this room; it has not been cleaned for some time and is in disorder, but it is not sordid or gloomy.

The back wall is a cloth with a door in the Centre. The side walls are not "solid," but consist each of two wings. Entrance from the street is up Right, up two steps, and along a nine-inch rostrum with a low banister. The rostrum ends at the door Centre, and gives one step down into the room. Continuing along the back wall, an exit above the up-stage wing, Left, leads to another room. (Right and Left being from the actors' point of view.) The upper Right wing is fitted with a shelf fitting; lower Right, painted with a skylight and a window, has practical pots and pans hooked to it. The upper Left wing is painted with another shelf fitting, long-handled brooms, boxes and trunks. The lower Left wing is built as a truck with a six-inch rostrum carrying an old dustbin, several boxes and a litter of pots and pans. Hooked to the wing are more pots and pans. The furniture consists of a rough desk up Left with a tall chair in front of it. A little lower Left stands a tall iron stove, with its

*pipe running up behind the border. Over on the Right
are two rough tables, one parallel with the banister,
the other running up and down stage, making an
inverted letter L. A rough chair stands by the upstage table and another behind the table Right. In
the corner down Right are a number of old boxes.
Centre stage is a trap door, the trap hinged to open
down stage. A low railing, the same length as the
trap, runs along its down-stage edge. Along the Left
edge stands a rough wooden bench with a low back,
its seat facing Left. A ladder runs down the trap to
the shop window. A large Gladstane bag is by the
desk. Joe Scanlon's small bag is up there too. Ambrose
Kemper's hat and coat are over Right, behind the
table.*

It is early morning.

VANDERGELDER, *60, choleric, vain and sly, wears a soiled
dressing gown over his uniform trousers; a check
cloth and white towel round his neck, seated in the
chair at the desk being shaved by* JOE SCANLON, *who
is Right of him.* VANDERGELDER *is smoking a cigar
and holding a hand mirror. He is in argument with*
AMBROSE KEMPER, *who, as the Curtain rises, walks
from up Centre to down Right.*

VANDERGELDER. Now listen, Mr. Kemper. I tell you for
the hundredth time you will never marry my niece.
AMBROSE. *(30, dressed as an "artist" crosses up Centre)*
And I tell you for the thousandth time that I will marry
your niece; and right soon, too
VANDERGELDER. *(Crosses up Right)* Never! Boys!
Boys! Go practice under somebody else's window.

*(*AMBROSE *crosses down Right around tables and up Centre again.* JOE *moves to Left of* VANDERGELDER.*)*

AMBROSE. Your niece is of age, Mr. Vandergelder. Your

niece has consented to marry me— This is a free country, Mr. Vandergelder—not a private kingdom of your own.

(JOE *shaving throat.* VANDERGELDER *rises, moves to the bench and sits.* JOE *follows.*)

VANDERGELDER. There are no free countries for fools, Mr. Kemper. Thank you for the honour of your visit— good morning. *(He moves his head.)*

(AMBROSE *sits Centre chair.*)

JOE. *(50; lanky, mass of gray hair falling into his eyes.* JOE *shaving throat)* Mr. Vandergelder, will you please sit still one minute. If I cut your throat it'll be practically unintentional.

VANDERGELDER. Ermengarde is not for you, nor for anybody else who can't support her.

AMBROSE. I tell you I can support her. *(Moves chair to bench)* I make a very good living.

VANDERGELDER. *(Crosses Right, below table)* No, sir! A living is made, Mr. Kemper, by selling something that everybody needs at least once a year.

AMBROSE. Yes but— *(Crosses Right Centre.)*

VANDERGELDER. Yes, sir! And a million is made by producing something that everybody needs every day. You artists produce something that nobody needs at any time.

AMBROSE. That's not true— *(Crosses down Right.)*

VANDERGELDER. You may sell a picture once in a while, but you'll make no living. *(Crosses around table to Right)* Joe, go over there and stamp three times. I want to talk to Cornelius.

(JOE *crosses below bench to trap door and replaces chair.*)

AMBROSE. Not only can I support her now, but I have considerable expectations. *(Crosses Right Centre.)*

VANDERGELDER. *Expectations!*

(JOE *stamps.* VANDERGELDER *stamps.*)

We merchants don't do business with them. I don't keep accounts with people who promise somehow to pay something some day, and I don't allow my niece to marry such people. No. No, Mr. Kemper.

(AMBROSE *crosses down Right.*)

(VANDERGELDER *sits on chair at desk and faces down stage.*) You go back to your studio and when you've finished painting your sunset on the Hudson, why don't you try 'Hope' feeding a family or how about 'Love' melting a snowbank? There is a subject for you.

(JOE *comes back above bench to Right of him.*)

AMBROSE. *(Going towards hat and coat, down Right. Crosses up Right Centre.)* Very well, from now on you might as well know that I regard any way we can find to get married is right and fair. *(Starts out. Turns. Crosses Centre.)* Ermengarde is of age, and there's no law—

VANDERGELDER. Law? *(Rises.)* Let me tell you something, Mr. Kemper; most of the people in the world are fools. The Law is there to prevent crime; we men of sense are there to prevent foolishness. *(Sits.)* It's I, and not the Law, that will prevent Ermengarde from marrying you, and I've taken some steps already. I've sent her away—

AMBROSE. You sent her away?

VANDERGELDER. Yes, to get this nonsense out of her head.

AMROSE. *(To Centre.)* Ermengarde's—not here!

VANDERGELDER. Oh, you can find her at Peekskill or Albany or try Syracuse or Utica. I thank you for the honor of your visit.

(AMBROSE *crosses Right.*)

GERTRUDE. *(Enters Left—70; deaf; half-blind; and very pleased with herself. She crosses to Right Centre and sits at the table.)* Everything's ready, Mr. Vandergelder. I have just finished packing the trunk. Ermengarde's been helping me. *(Ties two pieces of string together.)*

VANDERGELDER. Hold your tongue!

(JOE, *on the Right, is shaving* VANDERGELDER'S *throat, so he can only wave his hands vainly.*)

GERTRUDE. Yes, Mr. Vandergelder, Ermengarde's ready to leave. Her trunk's all marked. Care Miss Van Huysen, 8 Jackson Street, New York.

VANDERGELDER. *(Breaking away from* JOE*)* Hell and damnation! *(Crosses to Right Centre.)* Didn't I tell you it was a secret?

AMBROSE. *(Picks up hat and coat, kisses* GERTRUDE *and crosses to* VANDERGELDER.*)* Care Miss Van Huysen, 8 Jackson Street, New York. Thank you very much. Good morning, Mr. Vandergelder. *(Exits up Right.)*

VANDERGELDER. *(At Centre, calling after him)* It won't help you, Mr. Kemper— *(Crosses to* GERTRUDE.*)* Deaf! At least you can do me the favour of being dumb!

GERTRUDE. Chk—chk! Such a temper! Lord save us!

(CORNELIUS *puts his head through the trap-door. He is 33; mock-deferential—he wears a black apron and is in his shirt-sleeves.*)

CORNELIUS. Yes, Mr. Vandergelder?

VANDERGELDER. *(Right of trap door.)* Go in and get my niece's trunk and carry it over to the station.

CORNELIUS. Yes, Mr. Vandergelder.

VANDERGELDER. Wait! *(Crosses down to her.)* Gertrude, has Mrs. Levi arrived yet?

(CORNELIUS *crosses to trap, closes it.* JOE *strops razor at desk.*)

GERTRUDE. *(Loudly)* Don't shout. I can hear perfectly well. Certainly the labels for the luggage are ready. *(Exits Left with string.)*

VANDERGELDER. Have the buggy brought round to the

front of the store in half an hour. *(Sits on up stage table.)*
CORNELIUS. Yes, Mr. Vandergelder.

(JOE crosses and begins to shave his neck.)

VANDERGELDER. This morning I'm leading my Lodge
parade down to Spuyten Duyvil; this afternoon I'm
going to New York. Before I go, I have something im-
portant to say to you and Barnaby. Good news. Fact is—
I'm going to promote you. How old are you?
CORNELIUS. Thirty-three, Mr. Vandergelder.
VANDERGELDER. What?
CORNELIUS. Thirty-three.
VANDERGELDER. That all? That's a foolish age to be at.
I thought you were forty.
CORNELIUS. No, I'm thirty-three.
VANDERGELDER. A man's not worth a cent until he's
forty. We just pay 'em wages to make mistakes—don't we,
Joe? *(Turns head towards JOE.)*
JOE. You almost lost an ear on it, Mr. Vandergelder.
VANDERGELDER. I was thinking of promoting you to chief
clerk.
CORNELIUS. What am I now, Mr. Vandergelder?

(JOE uses neck brush.)

VANDERGELDER. You're an impertinent fool, that's what
you are. Now, if you behave yourself, I'll promote you from
impertinent fool to chief clerk, with a raise in your wages.
And Barnaby may be promoted from idiot apprentice to
incompetent clerk.
CORNELIUS. Thank you, Mr. Vandergelder.
VANDERGELDER. However, I want to see you again before
I go. Go in and get my niece's trunk.

(JOE removes apron and towel.)

CORNELIUS. Yes, Mr. Vandergelder. *(Exits Left.)*
VANDERGELDER. *(Crosses down to Left of bench, sits.)*

Joe—the world's getting crazier every minute. Like my father used to say: the horse'll be taking over the world soon.

(JOE *goes to desk for mirror, then down to Right of bench—presenting mirror.* VANDERGELDER *looks in mirror*)

Fi-fine!

JOE. I did what I could, Mr. Vandergelder, what with you flying in and out of the chair. (*Crosses up to desk, gathers equipment.*)

VANDERGELDER. Fine, fine. Joe, you do a fine job, the same fine job you've done me for twenty years. Joe— I've got special reasons for looking my best today—isn't there something a little extry you could do, something a little special?

JOE. Huh?

VANDERGELDER. I'll pay you right up to fifty cents—see what I mean? Do some of those things you do to the young fellas. Touch me up, smarten me up a bit. (*Hands mirror back.*)

JOE. (*Crosses to face him*) All I know is fifteen cents' worth, like usual, Mr. Vandergelder; and that includes everything that's decent to do to a man. (*He goes for his bag.*)

VANDERGELDER. Now hold your horses, Joe—all I meant was—

JOE. I've shaved you for twenty years and you never asked me no such questions before. And I don't intend—

(VANDERGELDER *rises, crosses to Left of* JOE. JOE *on to rostrum—making to go.*)

VANDERGELDER. (*Takes collar from desk and follows a step*) Hold your horses, I say, Joe! I'm going to tell you a secret. But I don't want you telling it to that riff-raff down to the barber shop what I'm going to tell you now. All I ask of you is a little extry because I'm thinking of getting married again; and this very afternoon I'm going to New York to call on my intended, a very refined lady. (*Moving away down Right Centre.*)

JOE. (*Off rostrum to Centre.*) Your gettin' married is none of my business, Mr. Vandergelder. I done everything to you I know, and the charge is fifteen cents like it always was, and—

(CORNELIUS *crosses Left to Right carrying a trunk on his shoulder.* ERMENGARDE *and* GERTRUDE *follow. They each put a wicker hamper on bench.* GERTRUDE *addresses a label at desk, then sits down stage on bench and ties label on larger hamper.*)

I don't dye no hair, not even for fifty cents I don't!

VANDERGELDER. Joe Scanlon, get out! (*Crosses below bench to Centre.*)

JOE. (*On rostrum again.*) And lastly, it looks to me like you're pretty rash to judge which is fools and which isn't fools, Mr. Vandergelder. People that's et onions is bad judges of who's et onions and who ain't— Good morning, ladies; good morning, Mr. Vandergelder. (*Exits up Right.*)

VANDERGELDER. The world's going crazy. The asylums can't hold them all. They're flooding the country. Well, what do you want? (*At Right, below table.*)

ERMENGARDE. (*Forward above bench to Right of desk —24; pretty, sentimental.*) Uncle! You said you wanted to talk to us.

VANDERGELDER. Oh yes, Gertrude, go and get my parade regalia,—the uniform for my Lodge parade.

GERTRUDE. (*Mumbles.*) What? Oh yes. Lord have mercy! (*Exits up Centre.*)

VANDERGELDER. Ermengarde. I had a talk with that artist of yours.

ERMENGARDE. Oh, you did?

VANDERGELDER. Yes I did. He's a fool.

(ERMENGARDE *starts to cry.*)

(VANDERGELDER *crosses to desk.*) Weeping! Weeping! You can go down and weep for a while in New York where it won't be noticed. (*He sits on desk chair.*) Ermengarde. Ermengarde! *(Motions her to him.)* I told him that when you were old enough to marry you'd marry some-one who could support you. I've done you a good turn. You'll come and thank me when you're fifty.

ERMENGARDE. But, Uncle, I love him!

VANDERGELDER. I tell you you don't.

ERMENGARDE. But I *do!*

VANDERGELDER. And I tell you you don't. Leave those things to me.

ERMENGARDE. If I don't marry Ambrose I know I'll die.

VANDERGELDER. What of?

ERMENGARDE. A broken heart.

VANDERGELDER. Never heard of it. Mrs. Levi is com-ing in a moment to take you to New York.

(GERTRUDE *re-enters Centre with sword, puts it on the hampers on bench and sits down stage on bench.* MALACHI STACK *enters up Right.)*

You are going to stay two or three weeks with Miss Van Huysen, an old friend of your mother's. You're not to receive any letters except from me. I'm coming to New York myself today and I'll call on you tomorrow. *(To* MALACHI.) Who are you?

MALACHI. *(On rostrum. 50; sardonic. Apparently inno-cent smile; pretense of humility.)* Malachi Stack, your honor. I heard you wanted an apprentice in the hay, feed, provision and hardware business.

VANDERGELDER. *(Rising and going down Right)* An apprentice at your age?

MALACHI. *(Removing hat and coming Centre)* Yes, your honor; I bring a lot of experience to it.

VANDERGELDER. Have you any letters of recommenda-tion?

MALACHI. *(Extending a sheaf of soiled papers)* Yes, indeed, your honor! First class recommendation.

VANDERGELDER. *(Crosses to below table Right.)* Ermen-garde! Are you ready to start?

ERMENGARDE. Yes.

VANDERGELDER. Well, go and get ready some more.

(She turns to go.)

Ermingarde! Let me know the minute Mrs. Levi gets here. *(He goes behind Right table.)*

(MALACHI *crosses down to face* VANDERGELDER.)

ERMINGARDE. Yes, Uncle Horace.

(ERMINGARDE *and* GERTRUDE *go out Left.)*

VANDERGELDER. *(Examines the letters; putting them down one by one.)* I don't want an able seaman. Nor a typesetter. And I don't want a hospital cook.

MALACHI. No, your honor, but it's all experience. Excuse me! *(Selects a letter.)* This one is from your former partner, Joshua Van Tuyl in Albany. *(He puts letters from table back into pocket.)*

VANDERGELDER. Oh, Van Tuyl! "—For the most part honest and reliable—occasionally willing and diligent." There seems to be a certain amount of hesitation about these recommendations.

MALACHI. Business men aren't writers, your honor. There's only one business man in a thousand that can write a good letter of recommendation, your honor. Mr. Van Tuyl sends his best wishes and wants to know if you can use me in the provision and hardware business.

VANDERGELDER. Not so fast, not so fast! *(Crossing below him to desk)* Tell me, why did you come to Yonkers?

MALACHI. *(Follows* VANDERGELDER.) I heard that you'd had an apprentice that was a good-for-nothing, and that you were at your wits' end for another.

VANDERGELDER. Wits' end, wits' end! There's no dearth of good-for-nothing apprentices.

MALACHI. That's right, Mr. Vandergelder. It's employers there's a dearth of. Seems like you hear of a new one dying every day.

VANDERGELDER. What's that? Hold your tongue. *(Sits at desk.)* I see you've been a barber, and a valet too. Why have you changed your place so often?

MALACHI. Changed my place, Mr. Vandergelder? When a man's interested in experience—

VANDERGELDER. Do you drink?

MALACHI. No, thanks. I've just had breakfast.

VANDERGELDER. I didn't ask you whether—idiot! I asked you if you were a drunkard.

MALACHI. No, sir! No! Why, looking at it from all sides I don't even like liquor.

VANDERGELDER. Well, if you keep on looking at it from all sides, out you go. Remember that. Here. *(Gives him remaining letters and moves down Right.)* With all your faults, I'm going to give you a try.

MALACHI. You'll never regret it, Mr. Vandergelder. You'll never regret it.

VANDERGELDER. Now today I want to use you in New York. I judge you know your way around New York?

MALACHI. *(A little nearer.)* Do I know New York? Mr. Vandergelder, I know every hole and corner in New York—

VANDERGELDER. *(Breaks in.)* Here's a dollar.

MALACHI. Thanks.

VANDERGELDER. *(Catches* MALACHI's *arm.)* A train leaves in a minute. Take that bag to the Central Hotel on Water Street, have them save me a room. Wait for me. I'll be there about four o'clock. *(Crosses to desk.)*

MALACHI. Yes, Mr. Vandergelder. *(Picks up the bag, starts out, then comes back.)* Oh, but first I'd like to meet the other clerks I'm to work with.

VANDERGELDER. You haven't time. Hurry now. The station's across the street.

MALACHI. Yes, sir. *(Away—then back once more.)* You'll see, sir, you'll never regret it—

VANDERGELDER. I regret it already. Go on. Off with you.

(MALACHI exits Right with bag.)

(Addresses the audience.) Ninety-nine percent of the people in the world are fools and the rest of us are in great danger of contagion. But I wasn't always free of foolishness as I am now. I was once young, which was

foolish; I fell in love, which was foolish; and I got married, which was foolish; and for a while I was poor, which was more foolish than all the other things put together. Then my wife died, which was foolish of her; I grew older which was sensible of me; then I became a rich man which is as sensible as it is rare. Since you see I'm a man of sense, I guess you were surprised to hear that I'm planning to get married again. Well, I've two reaons for it. In the first place, I like my house run with order, comfort and economy. That's a woman's work; but even a woman can't do it well if she's merely being paid for it. In order to run a house well, a woman must have the feeling that she owns it. Marriage is a bribe to make a housekeeper think she's a householder. Did you ever watch an ant carry a burden twice its size? What excitement! What patience! What will! Well, that's what I think of when I see a woman running a house. What giant passions in those little bodies—what quarrels with the butcher for the best cut—what fury at discovering a moth in a cupboard! Believe me!—If women could harness their natures to something bigger than a house and a baby-carriage—tck! tck!—they'd change the world. And the second reason, ladies and gentlemen? Well, I see by your faces you've guessed it already. There's nothing like mixing with women to bring out all the foolishness in a man of sense. And that's a risk I'm willing to take. I've just turned sixty and I've just laid side by side the last dollar of my first half-million. So if I should lose my head a little, I still have enough money to buy it back. *(He goes to behind the bench and picks up the sword.)* After many years' caution and hard work I have the right to a little risk and adventure, and I'm thinking of getting married. *(Goes towards Centre door.)* Yes, like all you other fools, I'm willing to risk a little security for a certain amount of adventure. Think it over. *(Exits up Centre.)*

*(*AMBROSE *enters up Right, crosses to Left and whistles softly. He wears hat but no overcoat.* ERMENGARDE*

enters Left and crosses to above bench. Puts hat on table.)

ERMENGARDE. Ambrose! *(Kiss.)* If my uncle saw you!

AMROSE. Sh! Get your hat.

ERMENGARDE. My hat!

AMBROSE. Quick! Your trunk's at the station. Now quick! We're running away.

ERMENGARDE. *(Loudly)* Running away!

AMBROSE. Sh!

ERMENGARDE. Where?

AMBROSE. To New York. To get married.

ERMENGARDE. Oh, Ambrose, I can't do that.

AMBROSE. Why?

ERMENGARDE. *(Sits down stage on bench.)* Ambrose dear—it wouldn't be proper!

AMBROSE. *(Kneels behind bench.)* Listen. I'm taking you to my friend's house. His wife will take care of you.

ERMENGARDE. But, Ambrose, a girl can't go on a train with a man. I can see you don't know anything about girls.

AMBROSE. But I'm telling you we're going to get married!

ERMENGARDE. Married! But what would *Uncle* say?

AMBROSE. We don't care—! We don't care what Uncle'd say—we're eloping.

ERMENGARDE. *(Rises, steps to Left and turns.)* Ambrose Kemper! How can you use such an awful word!

AMBROSE. *(Rises; steps back.)* Ermengarde, you have the soul of a field mouse.

ERMENGARDE. *(Crying)* Ambrose, why do you say such cruel things to me?

(MRS. LEVI *enters up Right. She stands listening.)*

AMBROSE. *(Steps forward.)* For the last time I beg you—get your hat and coat. The train leaves in a few minutes.

MRS. LEVI. *(Uncertain age; mass of sandy hair; impoverished elegance; large, shrewd but generous nature,*

*an assumption of worldly cynicism conceals a tireless,
amused enjoyment of life. She carries a handbag and a
small brown paper bag.)* Good morning, darling girl—
How are you? *(Crosses to* ERMINGARDE.)

(They kiss.)

ERMENGARDE. Oh, good morning, Mrs. Levi.

MRS. LEVI. And who is this gentleman who is so de-
voted to you? Huh?

ERMENGARDE. This is Mr. Kemper, Mrs. Levi. Ambrose,
this is—Mrs. Levi—

MRS. LEVI. Mrs. Levi, born Gallagher. Very happy to
meet you, Mr. Kemper. Mr. Kemper, *the artist!* Delighted! Mr. Kemper, may I say something very frankly?

AMBROSE. Yes, Mrs. Levi.

MRS. LEVI. This thing you were planning to do is a very
great mistake.

ERMENGARDE. Oh, Mrs. Levi, please explain to Ambrose
—of *course!* I want to marry him, but to *elope!*—How—

MRS. LEVI. Now, my dear girl, you go in and keep one
eye on your uncle. I wish to talk to Mr. Kemper for a
moment. You give us a warning when you hear your
Uncle Horace coming—

(ERMENGARDE *exits Centre.* AMBROSE *moves above
bench to stove.)*

(MRS. LEVI *crosses to down stage table, puts things on it.
Removes gloves.)* Mr. Kemper. I was this dear girl's
mother's oldest friend. Believe me. I am on your side. I
hope you two will be married very soon, and I think I can
say I can be of real *service* to you. Mr. Kemper, I always
go right to the point.

AMBROSE. What is the point, Mrs. Levi?

MRS. LEVI. Mr. Vandergelder is a very rich man, Mr.
Kemper, and Ermengarde is his only relative.

AMBROSE. *(Round above bench to her.)* Oh! But I am
not interested in Mr. Vandergelder's money. I have enough
to support a wife and family.

MRS. LEVI. Enough? How much is enough when one is

thinking about children and the future? The future is the most expensive luxury in the world, Mr. Kemper. *(Goes behind Right table.)*

AMBROSE. *(Brings other chair down and sits facing her across table.)* Mrs. Levi, what is the point?

MRS. LEVI. *(Dusts chair with paper bag. Sits.)* Believe me, Mr. Vandergelder wishes to get rid of Ermengarde, and if you follow my suggestions he will even permit her to marry you. You see, Mr. Vandergelder is planning to get married himself.

AMBROSE. What? That monster?

MRS. LEVI. Mr. Kemper!

AMBROSE. Married! To you, Mrs. Levi?

MRS. LEVI. Oh, no, no . . . No! I am merely arranging it. I am helping him find a suitable bride.

AMBROSE. For Mr. Vandergelder there are no suitable brides.

MRS. LEVI. I think we can safely say that Mr. Vandergelder will be married to someone by the end of next week.

AMBROSE. Well, what do you suggest, Mrs. Levi?

MRS. LEVI. I am taking Ermengarde to New York on the next train. I shall not take her to Miss Van Huysen's as is planned; I shall take her ' ᴐ my house. I wish you to call for her at my house at five-thirty. Here is my card. *(Rising, crosses below him to Centre.)*

AMBROSE. *(Has risen with her.)* "Mrs. Dolly Gallagher Levi. Varicose veins reduced."

MRS. LEVI. I beg your pardon—

AMBROSE. I beg your pardon; "Consultations Free."

MRS. LEVI. *(Takes bunch of cards from purse, goes through them.)* I meant to give you my other card. Here.

AMBROSE. "Mrs. Dolly Gallagher Levi. Aurora Hosiery. Instruction in the guitar and mandolin." You do all these things, Mrs. Levi? *(Sits on Right table.)*

MRS. LEVI. Two and two make four, Mr. Kemper— and they always did. So you will come to my house at five-thirty. At about six I shall take you both with me to the Harmonia Gardens Restaurant on the Battery; Mr.

Vandergelder will be there and everything will be arranged.

AMBROSE. How?

MRS. LEVI. Oh, I don't know. One thing will lead to another.

AMBROSE. How do I know that I can trust you, Mrs. Levi? You could easily make our situation worse.

MRS. LEVI. Mr. Kemper, your situation could not possibly be worse.

AMBROSE. I wish I knew what you get out of this, Mrs. Levi.

MRS. LEVI. That is a very proper question. I get two things: profit and pleasure.

AMBROSE. How?

MRS. LEVI. Mr. Kemper, I am a woman who arranges things. At present I am arranging Mr. Vandergelder's domestic affairs. Out of it I get—shall we call it: yes why don't we? Little pickings? I need little pickings, Mr. Kemper, and especially just now, when I haven't got my train-fare back to New York. You see: I am frank with you.

AMBROSE. That's your profit, Mrs. Levi; but where do you get your pleasure?

MRS. LEVI. My pleasure? Mr. Kemper, when you artists paint a hillside or a river you change everything a little, you make thousands of little changes, don't you? Nature is never completely satisfactory and must be corrected. Well, I'm like you artists. Life as it is is never quite interesting enough for me—I'm bored, Mr. Kemper, with life as it is—and so I do things. I put my hand in here, and I put my hand in there, and I watch and I listen—and often I am very much amused. *(Crosses Left.)*

AMBROSE. *(Rises, picks up hat.)* Not in my affairs, Mrs. Levi.

MRS. LEVI. Wait, I haven't finished. *(To Left Centre.)* There's another thing. I'm very interested in this household here—in Mr. Vandergelder and all that idle, frozen money of his. I don't like the thought of it lying in great piles, useless, motionless, in the bank, Mr. Kemper. Money should circulate like rain water. It should be flowing down among the people, through dressmakers and restaurants and cabmen, setting up a little business here, and furnishing a good time there. Do you see what I mean?

AMBROSE. Yes, I do.

MRS. LEVI. (*Crosses above bench to* AMBROSE.) New York should be a very happy city, Mr. Kemper, but it isn't. My late husband came from Vienna, Mr. Ephraim Levi: Oh my! now there's a city that understands this. I want New York to be more like Vienna and less like a collection of nervous and tired ants. And if you and Ermengarde get a good deal of Mr. Vandergelder's money, I want you to see that it starts flowing in and around a lot of people's lives.

ERMENGARDE. (*Enters up Centre. Down to bench.*) Mrs. Levi, Uncle Horace is coming.

MRS. LEVI. Mr. Kemper, I think you'd better be going—

(AMBROSE *takes hat, crosses below her to trap door and disappears down the ladder, closing trap as he goes.* ERMENGARDE *helps with trap.*)

(*As* AMBROSE *goes.*) Darling girl, Mr. Kemper and I have had a very good talk. You'll see: Mr. Vandergelder and I will be dancing at your wedding very, very soon—

(VANDERGELDER *enters Centre in full uniform and carrying a green banner; white gloves tucked in belt.*)

Oh, Mr. Vandergelder, how handsome you look!

(*He comes down to her.*)

You take my breath away.

(*They shake hands.*)

Yes, my dear girl, I'll see you soon. (*Takes her to Centre door.*)

(ERMENGARDE *exits Centre.* VANDERGELDER *crosses off platform, moves up Right, close to banister.*)

(*Left of him.*) Oh, Mr. Vandergelder, I wish Irene Molloy could see you now. But then! I don't know what's come over you lately. You seem to be growing younger every day.

VANDERGELDER. Allowing for exaggeration, Mrs. Levi. If a man eats careful there's no reason why he should look old.

MRS. LEVI. You never said a truer word.

VANDERGELDER. I'll never see sixty—er—fifty-five again.

MRS. LEVI. Fifty-five! Why, I can see at a glance that you're the sort that will be stamping about at a hundred—and eating five meals a day, just like what's-his-name—my Uncle Harry. At fifty-five my Uncle Harry was a mere boy—I'm a judge of hands, Mr. Vandergelder—show me your hand. *(Looks at it.)* Lord in heaven! What a life-line!

VANDERGELDER. Where?

MRS. LEVI. From *here* to *here*. It runs right off your hand. I don't know where it goes. *(Turns hand over. Looks up his sleeve.)* They'll have to hit you on the head with a mallet. They'll have to stifle you with a sofa pillow. You'll bury us all!

(VANDERGELDER *removes hat. She crosses and sits front of Right table. Handbag down.* VANDERGELDER *puts hat and gloves on desk and leans the banner against the wall.)*

However, to return to our business—Mr. Vandergelder I suppose you've changed your mind again. I suppose you've given up all idea of getting married.

VANDERGELDER. Not at all, Mrs. Levi. I have news for you.

MRS. LEVI. *(Bringing desk chair to Centre and standing behind it)* News?

VANDERGELDER. Mrs. Levi, I've practically decided to ask Mrs. Molloy to be my wife.

MRS. LEVI. You have?

VANDERGELDER. Yes, I have.

MRS. LEVI. Oh, you have! Well, I guess that's just about the best news I ever heard. Oh dear me! So there's nothing more for me to do but wish you every happiness under the sun and say goodbye.

VANDERGELDER. *(Stopping her)* Well—Mrs. Levi—Surely I thought—

MRS. LEVI. *(Going up Right again)* Well, I did have a little suggestion to make—but I won't. You're going to marry Irene Molloy and that closes the matter.

VANDERGELDER. What suggestion was that, Mrs. Levi?

MRS. LEVI. Well—I *had* found *another* girl for you.

VANDERGELDER. Another?

MRS. LEVI. The most wonderful girl, the ideal wife.

VANDERGELDER. Another, eh? What's her name? *(Turns.)*

MRS. LEVI. Her name?

VANDERGELDER. Yes!

MRS. LEVI. *(Crosses below table.)* Her name!—Ernestina—Simple. *Miss* Ernestina Simple. But now of course all that's too late. After all, you're engaged— *(Crosses Right.)* You're practically engaged to marry Irene Molloy.

VANDERGELDER. *(Crosses down Left, turns.)* Oh, I ain't engaged to Mrs. Molloy!

MRS. LEVI. Nonsense! You can't break poor Irene's heart now and change to another girl— *(Crosses Left Centre.)* When a man at your time of life calls four times on an attractive widow like that—and sends her a pot of geraniums, that's practically an engagement! *(Crosses Right.)*

VANDERGELDER. That ain't an engagement! *(Crosses up Left.)*

MRS. LEVI. And yet—! If only you were free! I've found this treasure of a girl. Every moment I felt like a traitor to Irene Molloy—but let me tell you: I couldn't help it. *(Sits.)* I told this girl all about you, just as though you were a free man. Isn't that dreadful? The fact is: she has fallen in love with you already.

VANDERGELDER. Ernestina?

MRS. LEVI. Ernestina Simple.

VANDERGELDER. *(Going round down to Left)* Ernestina Simple.

Mrs. Levi. Of course she's a very different idea from Mrs. Molloy, Ernestina is. Like her name— Simple, domestic, practical.

Vandergelder. Can she cook? *(Crosses Centre.)*

Mrs. Levi. Cook, Mr. Vandergelder? I've had two meals from her hands, and—as I live—I don't know what I've done that God should reward me with such meals.

(Vandergelder *goes to Right desk.*)
(She rises and comes to him.) I'm the best cook in the world myself, and I *know* what's good.

Vandergelder. Hm. How old is she, Mrs. Levi? *(Sits.)*

Mrs. Levi. Nineteen, well—say twenty. *(To behind up stage table.)*

Vandergelder. *(Rises. Following)* Twenty, Mrs. Levi? Girls of twenty are apt to favour young fellows of their own age. *(Perches on Left end of table.)*

Mrs. Levi. But you don't listen to me. And you don't know the girl. Mr. Vandergelder, she has a positive horror of flighty, brainless young men. A fine head of gray hair, she says, is worth twenty shined up with goose-grease.

Vandergelder. *(Crosses to Left.)* That's—that's not usual, Mrs. Levi.

Mrs. Levi. *(To him.)* Usual? I'm not wearing myself to the bone hunting up *usual* girls to interest you, Mr. Vandergelder. Usual, indeed. Listen to me. Do you know the sort of pictures she has on her wall? Is it any of these young Romeos and Lochinvars? No!—it's Moses on the mountain—that's what she's got. *(Crosses down Right Centre.)* If you want to make her happy, you give her a picture of Methuselah surrounded by his grandchildren. *(Sits.)* That's my advice to you.

Vandergelder. *(Above bench. Rests left foot on the bench.)* What's her family?

Mrs. Levi. Her father?—God be good to him! He was the best—what am I trying to say? Undertaker—the best undertaker in Brooklyn, respected, esteemed. He knew all the best people—knew them well, even before they died. So—well, that's the way it is. *(Rises. She comes over, takes his right arm and leads him down Left.)* Now let me tell you a little more of her appearance. Can you hear me: as I say, a beautiful girl, beautiful. I've seen her go down the street—you know what I mean?—the young men get dizzy. They have to lean against lampposts. And she? Modest eyes on the ground— I'm not going to tell you any more— *(Goes above bench to Centre, crosses back to down Right.)*

(VANDERGELDER follows her.)

Couldn't you come over to New York today?

VANDERGELDER. I was thinking of coming to New York this afternoon——

MRS. LEVI. You were? *(She turns.)* Well now, I wonder if something could be arranged— Oh, she's so eager to see you! Let me see—

VANDERGELDER. Could I— Mrs. Levi, could I give you two ladies a little dinner, maybe?

MRS. LEVI. Really, come to think of it, I don't see where I could get the time. I'm so busy over that wretched lawsuit of mine. Yes. If I win it, I don't mind telling you, I'll be what's called a very rich woman. I'll own half of Staten Island, that's a fact. But just now I'm at my wits' end for a little help, just enough money to finish it off. My wits' end! *(She looks in her handbag.)*

(In order not to hear this VANDERGELDER has a series of coughs, sneezes and minor convulsions. He moves over to desk. Replaces chair at desk.)

But perhaps I could arrange a little dinner; I'll see. *(Crosses to him.)* Yes, for that lawsuit all I need is fifty dollars, and Staten Island's as good as mine. I've been trotting all over New York for *you*, trying to find you a suitable wife.

VANDERGELDER. Fifty dollars!!

MRS. LEVI. Two whole months I've been—

VANDERGELDER. Fifty dollars, Mrs. Levi—is no joke. *(Producing purse, he turns half away from her.)* I don't know where money's gone to these days. It's in hiding— There's twenty—well, there's twenty-five. I can't spare no more, not now I can't.

(MRS. LEVI, *putting the notes away, goes below bench to Right Center. Sits at up stage table.* VANDERGELDER *crosses to her, Left.)*

MRS. LEVI. Well, this will help—will help somewhat. Now let me tell you what we'll do. I'll bring Ernestina to that restaurant on the Battery. You know it: the Harmonia Gardens. It's good, but it's not flashy. Now Mr. Vandergelder, I think it'd be nice if just this once you'd order a real nice dinner. I guess you can afford it.

VANDERGELDER. Well, just this once. *(Turns away.)*

MRS. LEVI. A chicken wouldn't hurt.

VANDERGELDER. *(Over Left shoulder. Crosses up Centre.)* Chicken!!—Well, just this once.

MRS. LEVI. And a little wine.

VANDERGELDER. *(Turns back.)* Wine? Well, just this once.

MRS. LEVI. Now about Mrs. Molloy—what do you think? Shall we call that subject closed?

VANDERGELDER. *(Turns and crosses above bench to down Left Centre.)* No, not at all, Mrs. Levi, I want to have dinner with—with Miss—

MRS. LEVI. Er—er—Simple!

VANDERGELDER. *(Crossing to her)* With Miss Simple; but first I want to make another call on Mrs. Molloy.

MRS. LEVI. *(Crossing below him towards Centre door)* Dear, dear, dear! And Miss Simple? What races you make me run! Very well! I'll meet you on one of those benches in front of Mrs. Molloy's hat store at four-thirty, as usual.

(Trap-door rises, and CORNELIUS's *head appears.)*

CORNELIUS. The buggy's here, ready for the parade, Mr. Vandergelder.

VANDERGELDER. Call Barnaby. I want to talk to both of you.

CORNELIUS. Yes, Mr. Vandergelder. *(Exit* CORNELIUS *down trap-door. Leaves trap open.)*

MRS. LEVI *(At Centre door.)* Now do put your thoughts

in order, Mr. Vandergelder. I can't keep upsetting and disturbing the finest women in New York City unless you mean business.

VANDERGELDER. (*Crossing to Left of her*) Oh, I mean business all right!

MRS. LEVI. I hope so. Because, you know, you're playing a very *dangerous* game.

VANDERGELDER. Dangerous?—Dangerous, Mrs. Levi?

MRS. LEVI. Of course, it's dangerous,—and there's a name for it! You're tampering with these women's affections, aren't you? And the only way you can save yourself now is to be married to *someone* by the end of next week. So think that over! (*Exits up Centre.*)

(*Enter* CORNELIUS *and* BARNABY *by the trap door.* BARNABY *to Right of trap,* CORNELIUS *to Left of bench.*)

VANDERGELDER. This morning I'm joining my lodge Parade, and this afternoon I'm going to New York. (*Look take.*) When I come back there are going to be some changes in the house. (*Crosses above trap and table to Right.*) I'll tell you what the change is, but I don't want you discussing it amongst yourselves—you're going to have a mistress.

BARNABY. (*17; round-faced, wide-eyed innocence; wearing a green baize apron. He looks at* CORNELIUS, *then at* VANDERGELDER.) I'm too young, Mr. Vandergelder!

VANDERGELDER. Not yours! Death and damnation! Not yours, idiot—mine! (*Then, realizing*) Hey! Hold your tongue until you're spoken to!

(BARNABY *moves to above table as* VANDERGELDER *crosses Centre.*)

I'm thinking of getting married.

CORNELIUS. (*Crosses above trap, hand outstretched.*) Many congratulations, Mr. Vandergelder, and my compliments to the lady.

VANDERGELDER. That's none of your business. Now go back to the store.

(The Boys *go down the ladder,* BARNABY *first.)*
(VANDERGELDER *crosses to down stage.)* Have you got
any questions you want to ask before I go?

CORNELIUS. Mr. Vandergelder—

VANDERGELDER. Yes—

CORNELIUS. Mr. Vandergelder—

VANDERGELDER. Yes, yes, Cornelius?

CORNELIUS. Does the chief clerk get one evening off
every week?

VANDERGELDER. So that's the way you begin being
chief clerk, is it? *(Crosses above trap, putting his gloves
on down Right.)* When I was your age I got up at five;
(Hat on.) I didn't close the shop until ten at night, and
then I put in a good hour at the account-books. The
world's going to pieces. You elegant ladies lie in bed until
six and at nine o'clock at night you rush to close the door
so fast the line of customers bark their noses. No, sir—
(To desk.) You'll attend to the store as usual, and on
Friday and Saturday nights you'll remain open until
ten—now hear what I say! *(Gloves on.)* This is the first
time I've been away from the store over-night. When I
come back I want to hear that you've run the place perfectly in my absence. If I hear of any foolishness, I'll
discharge you.

(BARNABY *falls.)*

An evening free! If you keep on asking for evenings free
you'll find yourself with all your days free! Remember
that! *(Takes banner and goes on rostrum. Signals band—
two beats.)* And don't forget to put the lid on the sheep
dip! *(Exits up Right.)*

BARNABY. *(To rostrum, watching him go.)* The horses
nearly ran away when they saw him. There he goes! Hoo-
hoo! *(Crosses Left and down.)* What's the matter, Cornelius?

CORNELIUS. *(Sits down stage end of bench.)* Chief
clerk! Promoted from chief clerk to chief clerk.

BARNABY. Don't you like it? *(Sits up stage of him on
bench.)*

CORNELIUS. Chief clerk!—and if I'm good, in ten years

I'll be promoted to chief clerk again. Thirty-three years old and I still don't get an evening free. When am I going to begin to live?

BARNABY. Well—eh—you can begin to live on Sundays, Cornelius.

CORNELIUS. That's not living. Twice to church, and old Wolf-Trap's eyes on the back of my head the whole time. And as for holidays! What did we do last Christmas? All those canned tomatoes went bad and exploded. We had to clean up the mess all afternoon. Was that living?

BARNABY. No.

CORNELIUS. (Rises.) Barnaby, how much money have you got—where you can get at it?

BARNABY. Oh—three dollars. Why, Cornelius?

CORNELIUS. You and I are going to New York.

BARNABY. Cornelius!!! (Rises.) We can't! Close the store?

CORNELIUS. Some more rotten tomatoes are going to explode.

BARNABY. Holy cabooses! How do you know?

CORNELIUS. I know they're rotten. All you have to do is to light a match under them. They'll make such a smell that customers can't come into the place for twenty-four hours. That'll get us an evening free. We're going to New York too, Barnaby, we're going to live! (Crosses below trap to down Right.) I'm going to have enough adventures to last me until I'm partner. So go and get your Sunday clothes on.

BARNABY. Wha-a-a-t? (Crosses above trap to COR-NELIUS.)

CORNELIUS. Yes, I mean it. We're going to have a good meal; and we're going to be in danger; and we're going to get almost arrested; and we're going to spend all our money.

BARNABY. Holy cab—

CORNELIUS. And one more thing: we're not coming back to Yonkers until we've kissed a girl. (Crosses Right.)

BARNABY. (Leans on table.) Kissed a girl! Cornelius, you can't do that. You don't know any girls.

CORNELIUS. I'm thirty-three. I've got to begin some time. *(At down Right.)*

BARNABY. I'm only seventeen, Cornelius. It isn't so urgent for me.

CORNELIUS. Don't start backing down now—if the worst comes to the worst and we get discharged from here we can always join the Army. *(Comes above tables to above trap.)*

BARNABY. *(Moving back as* CORNELIUS *comes forward)* Uh—did I hear you say that you'd be old Wolf-Trap's partner? *(Sits.)*

CORNELIUS. *(Leans against banister.)* How can I help it? He's getting old. If you go to bed at nine and open the store at six, you get promoted upwards whether you like it or not.

BARNABY. My! Partner!

CORNELIUS. Oh, there's no way of getting away from it. You and I will be Vandergelders.

BARNABY. I? Oh, no—I may rise a little, but I'll never be a Vandergelder.

CORNELIUS. *(Crosses down Centre.)* Listen—everybody thinks when he gets rich he'll be a different kind of rich person from the rich people he sees around him; later on he finds out there's only one kind of rich person, and he's it.

BARNABY. Oh, but I'll—

CORNELIUS. No. The best of all would be a person who has all the good things of a poor person, and all the good meals a rich person has, but that's never been known. No, you and I are going to be Vandergelders; all the more reason, then, for us to try and get some living and some adventure into us now—will you come, Barnaby?

BARNABY. But Wolf-Trap— Gert— Yes, Cornelius!

(Enter MRS. LEVI, ERMENGARDE *and* GERTRUDE *up Centre. The* BOYS *go down the ladder,* CORNELIUS *last.)*

MRS. LEVI. Mr. Hackl, is the trunk waiting at the railroad station?

CORNELIUS. Yes, Mrs. Levi. *(Closes the trap door.)*

MRS. LEVI. *(Coming Left of bench)* Take a last look, Ermengarde.

ERMENGARDE. What?

MRS. LEVI. Take a last look at your girlhood home, dear. I remember when I left my home. I gave a whinney like a young colt, and off I went.

(ERMENGARDE and GERTRUDE go off Right with two pieces of luggage.)

ERMENGARDE. *(As they go)* Oh Gertrude, do you think I ought to get married this way? A young girl has to be so careful!

MRS. LEVI. *(Down Centre. She addresses the audience.)* You know, I think I'm going to have this room with blue wallpaper,—yes, in blue! *(Hurries out after the OTHERS.)*

BARNABY. *(Comes up trap-door, looks off Right, then lies on floor Right of trap door.)* All clear up here, Cornelius! Cornelius—hold the candle steady a minute— the bottom row's all right—but try the top now—they're swelled up like they are ready to bust!

(BANG—revolver.)

Holy CABOOSES!

(BANG, BANG—revolver.)

Cornelius! I can smell it up here! *(Rises and goes towards Right; exits.)*

(Revolver SHOTS ad lib.)

CORNELIUS. *(Comes up trap and joins him.)* Get into your Sunday clothes, Barnaby. We're going to New York!

(As they run out there is a big explosion. A shower of tomato cans comes up from below followed by a billow of smoke as

THE CURTAIN FALLS

ACT TWO

Mrs. Molloy's hat store, New York City.

The back wall of the set contains a large wardrobe, Centre, with two doors to it. Left of the wardrobe is a recess which has the street door running up and down stage of its Left side. Right of the wardrobe, the counter runs up and down stage; and Right again, is the workroom door. Street and workroom doors have each a spring bell fitted. The Right wall is painted shelves with rolls of cloth and hats. The Left wall is the shop window. The floor of the window is built up on a four-inch rostrum, carrying a low brass rail in a half circle, with net curtain on rings. In the window is a large cane hatstand for display. At the up stage end of the rail stands a tall cheval mirror. Centre of the room, on a round carpet, is a large round table with a red cover which reaches to the floor. A small gilt chair is Left of the wardrobe and two tall bentwood chairs at the counter; on the table is a tray of ribbons, needles and cottons, also special flowers and chiffon to go on the boys' hats. Coats are in the wardrobe; hats are on and under the counter, on the table, and in the window.

As the Curtain rises, MRS. MOLLOY *is in the window, standing on a box, reaching up to put hats on the stand.* MINNIE FAY *is sewing by the counter.* MRS. MOLLOY *has a pair of felt overshoes, to be removed later.*

MRS. MOLLOY. Minnie, you're a fool. Of course I shall marry Horace Vandergelder.

MINNIE. Oh, Mrs. Molloy! I didn't ask you. I wouldn't dream of asking you such a personal question.

MRS. MOLLOY. Well, it's what you meant, isn't it? And there's your answer. I shall certainly marry Horace Vandergelder if he should ask me. *(Crawls under window-rail, singing loudly. Pushes box down stage. Crosses Right.)*

MINNIE. I know it's none of my business—

MRS. MOLLOY. *(Going around counter)* Speak up, Minnie. I can't hear you.

MINNIE. —but do you—do you—?

MRS. MOLLOY. *(Behind counter.)* Minnie, you're a fool. Say it: Do I love him? Of course, I don't love him. But I have two good reasons for marrying him just the same. *(Kneels and sings, gets hat with green and brown feathers.)* Minnie, put something on that hat. It's not ugly enough. *(Throws hat over counter.)*

MINNIE. *(Catching and taking hat to table)* Not ugly enough!

MRS. MOLLOY. I couldn't sell it. Put a—put a sponge on it.

MINNIE. *(Below table to Left of it.)* Why, Mrs. Molloy, you're in such a *mood* today.

MRS. MOLLOY. In the first place I shall marry Mr. Vandergelder to get away from the millinery business. I've hated it from the first day I had anything to do with it. Minnie, I hate hats. *(Sings loudly again as she crosses back of counter to window with three hats.)*

MINNIE. Why, what's the matter with the millinery business?

MRS. MOLLOY. I can no longer stand being suspected of being a wicked woman, while I have nothing to show for it. I just can't stand it. *(She crawls under rail into window.)*

MINNIE. Why, no one would dream of suspecting you.

MRS. MOLLOY. *(On her knes, she looks over the rail.)* Minnie, you're a fool. All millineresses are suspected of being wicked women. Why, half the time all those women come into the shop merely to look at me. *(Gets up.)*

MINNIE. Oh!

MRS. MOLLOY. *(Now placing hats on the stand)* They

enjoy the suspicion. But they aren't certain. If they were *certain* I was a wicked woman, they wouldn't put foot in this place again. Do I go to restaurants? No, it would be bad for business. Do I go to balls, or theatres, or operas? *(Places second hat down stage.)* No, it would be bad for business. The only men I ever meet are feather-merchants. *(Looks out. Crawls out of window. Closes drape.)* What are those two young men doing out there on that park bench?

(MINNIE *moves sewing tray to counter.*)

(Crosses above table, picks up hats from table.) Take my word for it, Minnie, either I marry Horace Vandergelder, or I break out of this place like a fire-engine. I'll go to every theatre and ball and opera in New York City. *(Back below counter, singing again.)*

MINNIE. *(Sitting down stage at counter)* But Mr. Vandergelder's not—

MRS. MOLLOY. Speak up, Minnie, I can't hear you.

MINNIE. —I don't think he's attractive.

MRS. MOLLOY. But what I think he is—and it's very important—I think he'd make a good fighter.

MINNIE. Mrs. Molloy!

MRS. MOLLOY. Take my word for it, Minnie: the best of married life is the fights. The rest is merely so-so.

MINNIE. *(Fingers in ears.)* I won't listen.

MRS. MOLLOY. *(One small hat in hand.)* Now Peter Molloy—God rest him!—was a fine arguing man. I pity the woman whose husband slams the door and walks out of the house at the beginning of an argument. Peter Molloy would stand up and fight for hours on end. He'd even throw things, Minnie, and there's no pleasure to equal that. When I felt tired I'd start a good blood-warming fight and it'd take ten years off my age; now Horace Vandergelder would put up a good fight; I know it. I've a mind to marry him. *(Kneels down to put hats under counter. Sings.)*

MINNIE. I think they're just awful, the things you're saying today. *(Crosses to window, fusses with a hat.)*

MRS. MOLLOY. Well, I'm enjoying them myself, too. *(Sings)*
  "So remember while you can
  What became of Nelly Ann,
  Who trusted in the promise of a drinking man."
MINNIE. *(At the window.)* Mrs. Molloy, those two men out in the street—
MRS. MOLLOY. What?
MINNIE. *(To table.)* Those men. It looks as if they meant to come in here.
MRS. MOLLOY. *(Below table to her.)* Well now, it's time some men came into this place. *(Raps her on bustle; turns her around.)* I give you the younger one, Minnie. *(Goes to table.)*
MINNIE. Aren't you terrible!

(MRS. MOLLOY *sits on Centre table, facing Left whilst* MINNIE *takes off her felt overshoes.)*

MRS. MOLLOY. Wait till I get my hands on that older one! Mark my words, Minnie, we'll get an adventure out of this yet. Adventure! Why does everybody have adventures except me, Minnie?
MINNIE. Mrs. Molloy!
MRS. MOLLOY. Because I have no spirit, I have no gumption. Minnie, they're coming in here. Let's go into the workroom and make them wait for us for a minute. *(Starts over Right.)*
MINNIE. Oh, but Mrs. Molloy—my work—! *(Takes sewing from table.)*
MRS. MOLLOY. *(Running to workroom)* Hurry up, Minnie. Be quick now.

(*They go out to workroom.* BARNABY *and* CORNELIUS *run in from street, leaving front door open.)*

BARNABY *(Left.)* No one's here.
CORNELIUS. *(Above table.)* Some women were here a minute ago. I saw them.

(They jump back to the street door and peer down the street.)

That's Wolf-Trap all right! *(Coming back above table)* Well, we've got to hide here until he passes by.

BARNABY. He's sitting down on that bench. It may be quite a while.

CORNELIUS. When these women come in, we'll have to make conversation until he's gone away. We'll pretend we're buying a hat. How much money have you got now?

BARNABY. *(Left, counting his money.)* Forty cents for the train—seventy cents for dinner—twenty cents to see the whale—and a dollar I lost—I have seventy cents.

CORNELIUS. And I have a dollar seventy-five. I wish I knew how much hats cost! *(Over by counter.)*

BARNABY. Is this an adventure, Cornelius?

CORNELIUS. No, but it may be.

BARNABY. I think it is. There we wander around New York all day and nothing happens; and then we come to the quietest street in the whole city and suddenly Mr. Vandergelder turns the corner. *(Going to door)* I think it's an adventure. I think— Cornelius! That Mrs. Levi is there now. She's sitting down on the bench with him.

CORNELIUS. *(Crosses above table to door.)* What do you know about that! We know only one person in all New York City, and there she is!

BARNABY. *(Closing door)* Even if our adventure came along now I'd be too tired to enjoy it. Cornelius, why isn't this an adventure?

CORNELIUS. *(Left of table to below it.)* Don't be asking that. When you're in an adventure, you'll know all right.

BARNABY. *(Left of table. Kneeling)* Maybe I wouldn't. Cornelius, let's arrange a signal for you to give me when an adventure's really going on.

(CORNELIUS *to up stage of window.*)

For instance, Cornelius, you say—uh—uh—*pudding!* You say *pudding* to me if it's an adventure we're in.

CORNELIUS. I wonder where the lady who runs this store is? What's her name again? *(Crosses Left, below table.)*

BARNABY. *(Below table. Rises; crosses Left Centre.)* "Mrs. Molloy, hats for ladies."

CORNELIUS. Oh yes. I must think over what I'm going to say when she comes in. *(To counter.)* "Good afternoon, Mrs. Molloy, wonderful weather we're having. We've been looking everywhere for some beautiful hats."

BARNABY. *(Left of table.)* That's fine, Cornelius!

CORNELIUS. "Good afternoon, Mrs. Molloy; wonderful weather—" We'll make her think we're very rich. *(One hand in trouser pocket, the other on back of chair.)*

   (BARNABY puts hands in trouser pockets.)

"Good afternoon, Mrs. Molloy—" You keep one eye on the door the whole time.

   (BARNABY goes to door.)

"We've been looking everywhere for—"

MRS. MOLLOY. *(Enters from the workroom.)* Oh, I'm sorry. *(Closing door)* Have I kept you waiting? Good afternoon, gentlemen.

CORNELIUS. *(Hat off.)* Here, Cornelius Hackl.

BARNABY. *(Hat off.)* Here, Barnaby Tucker.

MRS. MOLLOY. I'm very happy to meet you. Perhaps I can help you. Won't you sit down?

CORNELIUS. Thank you, we will.

   (Hats on table. They sit at the counter—CORNELIUS down stage.)

You see, Mrs. Molloy, we're looking for hats.

MRS. MOLLOY. Is that so?

CORNELIUS. We've looked everywhere. Do you know what we heard? "Go to Mrs. Molloy," they said. So we came here. *(Pause.)* Only place we could go—

MRS. MOLLOY. Well now, that's *very complimentary*.

CORNELIUS. —and we were right. Everybody was right.

MRS. MOLLOY. *(To BARNABY.)* You wish to choose some hats for a friend?

CORNELIUS. Yes, exactly. *(Kicks BARNABY.)*

BARNABY. Yes, exactly.

CORNELIUS. We were thinking of five or six, weren't we, Barnaby?

BARNABY. Er—five.

CORNELIUS. You see, Mrs. Molloy, money's no object with us. None at all.

MRS. MOLLOY. Why, Mr. Hackl—

CORNELIUS. *(Rises and goes toward street door. Turns.)* —I beg your pardon, what an interesting street! *(Continues up Left.)* Something happening every minute. Passersby, and—

(BARNABY *runs to join him. Kneels.)*

MRS. MOLLOY. *(Trying to make sensible conversation)* You're from out of town, Mr. Hackl?

CORNELIUS. *(Coming back)* Yes, Ma'am— Barnaby, just keep your eye on the street, will you? You won't see that in Yonkers every day.

BARNABY. *(Remains kneeling at street door.)* Oh yes, I will.

CORNELIUS. *(Turns.)* Not all of it.

MRS. MOLLOY. Now this friend of yours—couldn't she come in with you some day and choose her hats herself?

CORNELIUS. *(Sits up stage chair at counter.)* No. Oh, no. It's a surprise for her.

MRS. MOLLOY. Indeed? That may be a little difficult, Mr. Hackl. It's not entirely customary— Your friend's very interested in the street, Mr. Hackl.

CORNELIUS. Oh yes. Yes. He has a reason to be.

MRS. MOLLOY. You said you were from out of town?

CORNELIUS. Yes, we're from Yonkers.

MRS. MOLLOY. Yonkers?

CORNELIUS. Yonkers— *(Drops gaze.)* Yes, Yonkers. You should know Yonkers, Mrs. Molloy. Hudson River; Palisades; drives; some say it's the most beautiful town in the world; that's what they say.

MRS. MOLLOY. Is that so?

CORNELIUS. *(Rises.)* Mrs. Molloy, if you ever had a Sunday free, I'd—we'd like to show you Yonkers. Y'know, it's very historic, too.

MRS. MOLLOY. That's very kind of you. Well, perhaps—

Now about those hats. *(Holding gaze, takes two hats from under counter, a yellow straw with cherry and green straw with feather. Crosses below table to above it.)*

CORNELIUS. *(Following)* Is there— Have you a— Maybe Mr. Molloy would like to see Yonkers too?

MRS. MOLLY. *(Turns to him.)* Oh, I'm a widow, Mr. Hackl.

CORNELIUS. *(Turns back and picks up hat on top of box.)* You are! *(Steps up stage.)* Oh, that's too bad. *(Steps down stage to up Centre of table; puts hats on table.)* Mr. Molloy would have enjoyed Yonkers.

MRS. MOLLOY. Very likely. Now this friend of yours, Mr. Hackl, is she light or dark?

CORNELIUS. *(Below table to Right of it.)* Don't think about that for a minute. Any hat you'd like would be perfectly all right with her.

MRS. MOLLOY. Really! *(She puts one on. Turns to him.)* Do you like this one?

CORNELIUS. Barnaby! *(Crosses above table behind MRS. MOLLOY to him.)* Barnaby! Look!

(BARNABY turns, smiles, gives CORNELIUS a look and turns to door again.)

BARNABY. Oh that's fine.

CORNELIUS. Mrs. Molloy, that's the most beautiful hat I ever saw.

(Pause. BARNABY now crawls under the rail into the window.)

MRS. MOLLOY. Your friend is acting very strangely, Mr. Hackl.

CORNELIUS. Barnaby, stop acting strangely. When the street's quiet and empty, come back and talk to us. What was I saying? Oh yes: Mrs. Molloy, you should know Yonkers.

MRS. MOLLOY. *(Hat off. To table; picks up two hats.)* The fact is, I have a friend in Yonkers. Perhaps you know

him. It's always so foolish to ask in cases like that, isn't
it?

> (BOTH *laugh over this with increasing congeniality.*
> MRS. MOLLOY *goes to counter with hats from table.*
> CORNELIUS *follows.*)

(At counter with back to him, putting down hats.) It's a
Mr. Vandergelder.

> (BARNABY, *in window, head up.*)

CORNELIUS. *(Stops abruptly.)* What was it you said?
MRS. MOLLOY. *(Turns.)* Then you do know him?
CORNELIUS. Horace Vandergelder?
MRS. MOLLOY. Yes, that's right.
CORNELIUS. Know him! *(Look to BARNABY.)* Why, no.
No!
BARNABY. No. No.
CORNELIUS. I beg your pardon, Mrs. Molloy—what an
attractive shop you have! *(Smiling fixedly at her he
moves to the workshop door.)* And where does this door
lead to? *(Opens it.)*
MRS. MOLLOY. Why, Mr. Hackl, that's my workroom.
(Pushes chair out of way.)
CORNELIUS. Everything here is so interesting. *(Looks
under counter.)* Every door. Every corner, Mrs. Molloy.
Barnaby, notice the interesting doors and cupboards.
(He opens the Right wardrobe door.) Deeply interesting.
Coats for ladies. *(Laughs.)* Barnaby, make a note of the
table. Precious piece of furniture, with a low-hanging
cloth, I see. *(Stretches his leg under table.)*
MRS. MOLLOY. *(Crosses up Centre, taking a hat from
box Left of wardrobe. Puts hat on table; turns back with
lid and puts it on box.)* Perhaps your friend might like
some of this new Italian straw. Mr. Vandergelder's a very
substantial man and very well liked, they tell me. *(Puts
empty box on up stage end of counter.)*
CORNELIUS. *(Sits down stage chair at counter.)* A
lovely man, Mrs. Molloy.
MRS. MOLLOY. Oh yes—charming, charming!

CORNELIUS. *(Smiling sweetly)* Has only one fault, as far as I know: he's hard as nails; but apart from that, as you say, a charming nature, ma'am.

MRS. MOLLOY. *(Back to table.)* And a large circle of friends—? *(She pins loose ribbon to back of hat.)*

CORNELIUS. Yes, indeed,—five or six.

(MRS. MOLLOY turns to mirror, putting on hat.)

BARNABY. *(Head up.)* Five!

CORNELIUS. *(Rises; to above table.)* He comes and calls on you here from time to time, I suppose.

MRS. MOLLOY. *(Puts hat on at mirror. Turns from mirror to Centre.)* This summer we'll be wearing ribbons down our backs. *(Pause.)* Yes, as a matter of fact I am expecting a call from him this afternoon. *(Hat off.)*

BARNABY. *(Getting to his feet)* I think— Cornelius! I think—!!

MRS. MOLLOY. *(Turns to window. Drops hat behind rail.)* Now to show you some more hats—

BARNABY. Look out! *(He takes a flying leap over the rail and flings himself under the table.)*

(MRS. MOLLOY drops hat over window rail and runs above table.)

CORNELIUS. Begging your pardon, Mrs. Molloy. *(He jumps into the wardrobe, using Left door.)*

MRS. MOLLOY. *(Runs after him; stops at door; knocks.)* Gentlemen! Mr. Hackl! Come right out of there this minute!

CORNELIUS. Help us just this once, Mrs. Molloy! We'll explain later! *(Closes door.)*

MRS. MOLLOY. *(Knocks.)* Mr. Hackl!

BARNABY. We're as innocent as can be, Mrs. Molloy.

MRS. MOLLOY. *(Claps hands.)* Come out of there. *(Bangs on wardrobe door again.)* But really! Gentlemen! I can't have this! *What are you doing? (Closes door, turns down stage. Turns to look at* BARNABY.*)*

BARNABY. Cornelius! Cornelius! Pudding?

*(CORNELIUS opens Left door, which hits MRS. MOLLOY
in the back.)*

CORNELIUS. Pudding!

*(They disappear from sight—CORNELIUS in wardrobe,
BARNABY under table. Enter MRS. LEVI followed by
VANDERGELDER. MRS. LEVI crosses to MRS. MOLLOY.
VANDERGELDER goes down Left. He carries a large
box of sweets and walking stick.)*

MRS. LEVI. Irene, my darling child, how are you?
Heaven be good to us, how well you look!

(They kiss.)

MRS. MOLLOY. But what a surprise! And Mr. Vandergelder in New York—what a pleasure! *(Goes above table
to him.)*
VANDERGELDER. *(Swaying back and forth on his heels
complacently, bows)* Good afternoon, Mrs. Molloy.

*(They shake hands. MRS. MOLLOY brings chair from
counter for him to below table.)*

MRS. LEVI. Yes, Mr. Vandergelder's in New York.
Yonkers lies up there—*decimated* today. Irene, we
thought we'd pay you a very short call. *(To up stage
Centre.)* Now you'll tell us if it's inconvenient, won't you?
MRS. MOLLOY. *(Placing a chair Right of table for MRS.
LEVI)* Inconvenient, Dolly! The idea! Why, it's sweet
of you to come. *(She notices the boys' hats on the up
stage table—sticks a spray of flowers into crown of COR-
NELIUS'S; puts ribbon around BARNABY'S. Puts dent in,
then steps back, looks at hats.)*
VANDERGELDER. We waited outside a moment.

MRS. LEVI. Mr. Vandergelder thought he saw two customers coming in—two men.

MRS. MOLLOY. *(Up Centre of table. Picks up hat; puts it down again.)* Men! Men, Mr. Vandergelder? Why, what will you be saying next?

MRS. LEVI. *(Facing downstage)* Then we'll sit down for a minute or two— (MRS. LEVI *goes to sit down in chair Right of table.)*

(During the following dialogue this business takes place: MRS. MOLLOY pulls the chair from under MRS. LEVI, who clutches the table cover and partly pulls it off. VANDERGELDER puts his hat and the sweets box on the Left edge of the table. MRS. MOLLOY runs over to get him into the workroom. As they reach the counter, BARNABY pulls the table cover down on the Left side, making the hat and sweets box fall to the floor. VANDERGELDER runs back, picks box up, and is hustled into the workroom by MRS. MOLLOY, who shouts her last line loudly into the room and slams the door. She picks up chair and drags it to counter. MRS. LEVI on floor. VANDERGELDER re-enters. She goes to him, pulling tablecloth straight behind him; pushes him to Left of table as he comes to get hat. She goes behind him and pushes him out again.)

MRS. MOLLOY. Before you sit down, there's something I want to show you. I want to show Mr. Vandergelder my workroom, too.

MRS. LEVI. *(Rises.)* I've seen the workroom a hundred times. I'll stay right here and try on some of these hats.

MRS. MOLLOY. No, Dolly, you come too. I have something for you. Come along, everybody.

(MRS. LEVI *exits to workroom.)*

Mr. Vandergelder, I want your advice. You don't know how helpless a woman in business is. Oh, I feel I need advice every minute from a fine business head like yours.

(VANDERGELDER *exits to workroom.)*

Now I shut the door! (MRS. MOLLOY *exits to workroom.)*

CORNELIUS. *(Puts his head out of the Left door of wardrobe and gradually comes out into the room, leaving door open.)* Hsst!

BARNABY. *(Pokes his head out—Right side.)* Maybe she wants us to go, Cornelius?

CORNELIUS. Certainly I won't go. Mrs. Molloy would think we were just foolish fellows. No, all I want is to stretch a minute.

BARNABY. What are we going to do when Mr. Vandergelder goes, Cornelius?

CORNELIUS. Well—I don't know yet. I like Mrs. Molloy a lot. I wouldn't like her to think badly of me. I think I'll buy a hat. We can walk home to Yonkers, even if it takes us all night. I wonder how much hats cost. Barnaby, give me all the money you've got. *(As he leans over to take the money, he sneezes.)*

> (BOTH *return to their hiding places in alarm; then emerge again,* CORNELIUS *leaving Left door open again.)*

My, all those perfumes in that cupboard tickle my nose! (CORNELIUS *is facing wardrobe.)* But I like it in there—It's a woman's world, and very different.

BARNABY. I like it where I am, too; only I'd like it better if I had a pillow.

CORNELIUS. *(Taking coat from wardrobe)* Here, take one of these coats. I'll roll it up for you so it won't get mussed. Ladies don't like to have their coats mussed.

BARNABY. That's fine. Now I can just lie here and hear Mr. Vandergelder talk.

CORNELIUS. *(Goes slowly above table toward cheval mirror, repeating* MRS. MOLLOY's *line dreamily.)* This summer we'll be wearing ribbons down our back—

BARNABY. Can I take my shoes off, Cornelius?

CORNELIUS. *(Does not reply. He comes to the footlights and addresses the audience.)* Isn't the world full of wonderful things? There we sit cooped up in Yonkers years and years and all the time wonderful people like Mrs. Molloy are walking around in New York and we don't know them at all. *(He brings Left chair forward*

and sits.) I don't know whether—from where you're sitting—you can see—well, for instance, the way *(He points
to the edge of his right eye.)* her eye and forehead and
cheek come together, up here. Can you? And the kind
of fireworks that shoot out of her eyes all the time.
(Rises.) I tell you right now; a fine woman is the great-
est work of God. You can talk all you like about Niagara
Falls and the Pyramids; they aren't in it at all. Of course,
up there at Yonkers they came into the store all the time,
and bought this and that, and I said, "Yes, ma'am" and
"That'll be seventy-five cents, ma'am"; and I *watched*
them. But today I've talked to one, equal to equal, equal
to equal, and to the finest one that ever existed in my
opinion. *(Steps forward.)* They're so different from men!
Why, everything that they say and do is so different that
you feel like laughing all the time. *(He laughs.)* Golly,
they're different from men. *(Right knee on chair.)* And
they're awfully mysterious too. You never can be really
sure what's going on in their heads. They have a kind of
wall around them all the time—of pride, and a sort of
play-acting; I bet you could know a woman a hundred
years without ever being really sure whether she liked
you or not. *(Sits facing workroom—then turns.)* This
minute I'm in danger. I'm in danger of losing my job and
my future and everything that people think is important;
but I don't care. Even if I have to dig ditches for the rest
of my life, I'll be a ditch-digger who once had a wonderful
day. *(He puts chair back and goes Right of table.)*
Barnaby!

BARNABY. Oh, you woke me up! *(Puts head out.)*

CORNELIUS. *(Kneels.)* Barnaby, we can't go back to
Yonkers yet and you know why?

BARNABY. Why not?

CORNELIUS. We've had a good meal. We've had an
adventure. We've been in danger of getting arrested.
There's only one more thing we've got to do before we go
back to be successes in Yonkers.

BARNABY. Cornelius! You're never going to kiss Mrs.
Molloy!

CORNELIUS. Maybe.

BARNABY. But she'll scream.

CORNELIUS. Barnaby, you don't know anything at all. You might as well know right now that everybody except us goes through life kissing right and left all the time.

BARNABY. *(Pauses for reflection; humbly)* Well, thanks for telling me, Cornelius.

(CORNELIUS *rises.*)

I often wondered.

MRS. LEVI. *(Enters from workroom.)* Just a minute, Irene. I must find my handkerchief. *(She closes the door behind her.)*

(BARNABY *ducks back under table.* CORNELIUS *drops to his hands and knees and crawls slowly—as though to make himself invisible—to the wardrobe.* MRS. LEVI, *leaning over the counter, watches him in silence. Finally from the wardrobe* CORNELIUS *puts his head out and looks pleadingly at her.)*

Why, Mr. Hackl, I thought you were up to Yonkers.

CORNELIUS. *(To counter.)* I almost always am, Mrs. Levi. Oh, Mrs. Levi, don't tell Mr. Vandergelder! I'll explain everything later.

BARNABY. *(Head out.)* We're terribly innocent, Mrs. Levi.

MRS. LEVI. Why, who's that?

BARNABY. Barnaby Tucker, just paying a call.

MRS. LEVI. *(Looking under counter)* Well, who else is here?

CORNELIUS. Just the two of us, Mrs. Levi, that's all

MRS. LEVI. Old friends of Mrs. Molloy's, is that it?

CORNELIUS. We never knew her before a few minutes ago, but we like her a lot,—don't we, Barnaby? *(Steps down; faces up toward workroom.)* In fact, I think she's —I think she's the finest person in the world. I'm ready to tell that to anybody.

MRS. LEVI. And does she think *you're* the finest person in the world?

CORNELIUS. Oh no, I don't suppose she even notices that I'm alive.

MRS. LEVI. Well, I think she must notice that you're alive in that cupboard, Mr. Hackl. Well, if I were you I'd get back into it right away. Somebody could be coming in any minute.

(CORNELIUS *disappears.* MRS. LEVI *sits unconcernedly in Right chair.*)

MRS. MOLLOY. *(Enters, leaving door open.)* Can I help you, Dolly?
MRS. LEVI. No, no, no. I was just blowing my nose.
VANDERGELDER. *(Enters from workroom.)* Mrs. Molloy, I've got some advice to give you about your business.

(MRS. MOLLOY *puts* BARNABY's *hat on floor in window, then* CORNELIUS's *hat on counter, up stage end.*)

MRS. LEVI. Oh, advice from Mr. Vandergelder! The whole city should hear this.
VANDERGELDER. In the first place, the aim of business is to make profit.
MRS. MOLLOY. *(At counter.)* Is that so?
MRS. LEVI. I never heard it put so clearly before. Did you hear it?
VANDERGELDER. You pay those girls of yours too much. You pay them as much as men. Girls like that enjoy their work. Wages, Mrs. Molloy, are paid to make people do work they don't want to do. *(Crosses down and Left.)*
MRS. LEVI. Mr. Vandergelder thinks so ably. And that's exactly the way his business is run up in Yonkers.

(MRS. MOLLOY *goes to above table.*)

VANDERGELDER. Mrs. Molloy, I'd like for you to come up to Yonkers.
MRS. MOLLOY. That would be very nice.
   (He hands her the box of sweets.)
Oh thank you. As a matter of fact, I know someone from Yonkers, someone else. *(Puts candy on table.)*

VANDERGELDER. *(Hangs hat on down stage leg of cheval mirror.)* Oh? Who's that?

(MRS. MOLLOY *puts sweets on table and brings gilt chair forward.* VANDERGELDER *helps her and she sits above table.* VANDERGELDER *sits Left of table.)*

MRS. MOLLOY. Someone quite well-to-do, I believe, though a little free and easy in his behavior. Mr. Vandergelder, do you know Mr. Cornelius Hackl in Yonkers?

VANDERGELDER. Cornelius Hackl? I know him like I know my own boot. He's my head clerk.

MRS. MOLLOY. Is that so?

VANDERGELDER. He's been in my store for ten years.

MRS. MOLLOY. Well, I never!

VANDERGELDER. Where would you have known him?

(MRS. MOLLOY *is silent—looks at* MRS. LEVI, *nonplussed.)*

MRS. LEVI. Err—blah—err! Er—oh, just one of those chance meetings, I suppose.

MRS. MOLLOY. Yes, oh yes! One of those chance meetings.

VANDERGELDER. What? Chance meetings? Cornelius Hackl has no right to chance meetings. Where was it?

MRS. MOLLOY. Really, Mr. Vandergelder, it's very unlike you to question me in such a way. I think Mr. Hackl is better known than you think he is.

VANDERGELDER. Nonsense.

MRS. MOLLOY. He's in New York often, and he's very well liked.

MRS. LEVI. Well, the truth might as well come out now as later.

(MRS. MOLLOY *rises in alarm to up Centre; a look at wardrobe.)*

Mr. Vandergelder, Irene is quite right. Your head clerk is often in New York. Goes everywhere; has an army of friends. Everybody knows Cornelius Hackl.

VANDERGELDER. *(Laughs.)* He never comes to New York. He works all day in my store and at nine o'clock at night he goes to sleep in the bran room.

MRS. LEVI. So you think. But it's not true.

VANDERGELDER. Dolly Gallagher, you're crazy.

MRS. LEVI. Listen to me. You keep your nose so deep in your account books you don't know what goes on. Yes, by day, Cornelius Hackl is your faithful, trusted clerk— that's true; but by night! Well, he leads a double life, that's all! He's here at the opera; at the great resaurants; in all the fashionable homes—

(MRS. MOLLOY *brings chair above* MRS. LEVI *and sits.)*

—why, he's at the Harmonia Gardens Restaurant three nights a week. The fact is, he's the wittiest, gayest, naughtiest, most delightful man in New York. Well, he's just *the* famous Cornelius Hackl!

VANDERGELDER. It ain't the same man. If I ever thought Cornelius Hackl came to New York, I'd discharge him.

MRS. LEVI. Who took the horses out of Jenny Lind's carriage and pulled her through the streets?

MRS. MOLLOY. Who?

MRS. LEVI. Cornelius Hackl! Who dressed up as a waiter at the Fifth Avenue Hotel the other night and took an oyster and dropped it right down Mrs.— *(Rises; to counter.)* No, it's too wicked to tell you!

MRS. MOLLOY. *(Moves her chair back to its place; moves back to* MRS. LEVI.) Oh yes, Dolly, tell it! Go on!

MRS. LEVI. No. But it *was* Cornelius Hackl.

VANDERGELDER. It ain't the same man. Where'd he get the money?

MRS. LEVI. But he's very rich.

VANDERGELDER. Rich! I keep his money in my own safe. He has a hundred and forty-six dollars and thirty-five cents.

MRS. LEVI. *(Rises; to above table to him.)* Oh, Mr. Vandergelder, you're killing me! Do come to your senses. He's one of *the* Hackls.

(MRS. MOLLOY *sits where* MRS. LEVI *was.*)

VANDERGELDER. *The* Hackls? *(Rises.)*
MRS. LEVI. They built the Raritan Canal. *(She turns above table. Brings down chair.)*
VANDERGELDER. Then why should he work in my store?
MRS. LEVI. Well, I'll tell you. *(Sits above table.)*
VANDERGELDER. *(Walking around in a circle)* I don't want to hear! I've got a headache! I'm going home. *It ain't the same man!* He sleeps in my bran room. You can't get away from facts. I just made him my chief clerk.
MRS. LEVI. If you had any sense you'd make him partner. *(Rises; crosses to* MRS. MOLLOY.*)* Now Irene, I can see you were as taken with him as everybody else is.

(VANDERGELDER *crosses up Centre.*)

MRS. MOLLOY. Why, I only met him once, very hastily.
MRS. LEVI. Yes, but I can see that you were taken with him. Now don't you be thinking of marrying him!
MRS. MOLLOY. *(Her hands on her cheeks.)* Dolly! What are you saying? Oh!
MRS. LEVI. Maybe it'd be fine. But think it over carefully. He breaks hearts like hickory nuts.
VANDERGELDER. Who?
MRS. LEVI. *(Crossing above table to up Left)* Cornelius Hackl!
VANDERGELDER. *(Above table to her.)* Mrs. Molloy, how often has he called on you?
MRS. MOLLOY. *(Below table to down Left.)* Mr. Vandergelder, I'm telling the truth. I've only met him once in my life. Dolly Levi's been exaggerating so. I don't know where to look! *(Very pleased, she sways about, humming to herself, facing Left.)*

(MINNIE *enters from workroom—below table to hat-stand.* VANDERGELDER *sits by counter.*)

MINNIE. Excuse me, Mrs. Molloy. I must get together

that order for Mrs. Parkington. *(Takes hat from down stage of stand.)*

MRS. MOLLOY. Yes, we must get that off before closing.

MINNIE. I want to send it off by the errand girl. *(Goes above table to wardrobe.)* Oh, I almost forgot the coat.

MRS. MOLLOY. *(Running below table)* Oh, oh! I'll do that, Minnie!

(But she is too late. MINNIE opens the Right-hand cupboard door and falls back in terror and screams.)

MINNIE. Oh, Mrs. Molloy! Help! There's a man!

(MRS. MOLLOY, with the following speech, pushes her back to the workroom door. MINNIE walks with one arm pointing at the cupboard. At the end of each of MRS. MOLLOY's sentences she repeats—at the same pitch and degree—the words: "But there's a man!")

MRS. MOLLOY. *(Slamming wardrobe door)* Minnie, you imagined it. You're tired, dear. You go back in the workroom and lie down. Minnie, you're a fool! Hold your tongue!

MINNIE. But, there's a man! *(Exits to workroom.)*

(MRS. MOLLOY returns to below counter. VANDERGELDER goes down Right and raises his stick threateningly.)

VANDERGELDER. If there's a man there, we'll get him out. Whoever you are, come out of there! *(Strikes table with his stick as he crosses down Left.)*

MRS. LEVI. *(Goes masterfully to the wardrobe and sweeps her umbrella around among the coats.)* Nonsense! There's no man there. See? Miss Fay's nerves have been playing tricks on her. Come now, let's sit down again. What were you saying, Mr. Vandergelder?

(They sit—MRS. MOLLOY Right, MRS. LEVI Centre, VANDERGELDER Left. A sneeze is heard from the cup-

board. ALL *rise, look toward wardrobe, then sit
again.)*

MRS. LEVI. Well now—
(Another tremendous sneeze.)
(With a gesture that says "I can do no more.") God
bless you!

(ALL *rise.* VANDERGELDER *to below table.* MISS LEVI *to
up Centre.* MRS. MOLLOY *runs to the cupboard, then
to Right of table.)*

MRS. MOLLOY. *(To* VANDERGELDER.) Yes, there is a
man in there. *(Drags chair back to up stage of counter.)*
I'll explain it all to you another time. Thank you very
much for coming to see me. Good afternoon, Dolly. Good
afternoon, Mr. Vandergelder.
VANDERGELDER. You're protecting a man in there!
MRS. MOLLOY. *(With back to cupboard)* There's a
very simple explanation, but for the present, good afternoon.

(BARNABY *now sneezes twice, lifting the table each time.*
VANDERGELDER, *Right of table, jerks off the tablecloth.* BARNABY *pulls cloth under table and rolls himself up in it.* MRS. MOLLOY *picks up candy box from
floor.)*

MRS. LEVI. *(Coming down Left)* Lord, the room's
crawling with men! I'll never get over it. *(To up Left
again.)*
VANDERGELDER. The world is going to pieces! I can't
believe my own eyes! *(Crosses to Left to up Left Centre.)*
MRS. LEVI. Come, Mr. Vandergelder. Ernestina Simple
is waiting for us.
VANDERGELDER. *(To below table for hat; puts it on.)*
Mrs. Molloy, I shan't trouble you again, and *vice versa.*

(MRS. MOLLOY *is standing transfixed in front of ward-*

robe clasping the sweets box. VANDERGELDER *snatches the box from her and goes out.)*

MRS. LEVI. *(Crosses to her—kiss.)* Irene, when I think of all the interesting things you have in this room. Make the most of it, dear. *(Raps wardrobe.)* Goodbye! *(Raps on table with umbrella.)* Goodbye! *(Exits.)*

(MRS. MOLLOY *opens Left door of wardrobe.* CORNELIUS *steps out.* BARNABY *crawls to Right from under the table, still with cloth over him.)*

MRS. MOLLOY. So that was one of your practical jokes, Mr. Hackl!

CORNELIUS. No, no, Mrs. Molloy!

MRS. MOLLOY. Come out from that, Barnaby Tucker, you trouble-maker! *(She snatches the cloth and spreads it back on table.)*

     (MINNIE *enters to below counter.)*

There's nothing to be afraid of, Minnie. I know all about these gentlemen. You think because you're rich you can make up for all the harm you do, is that it?

CORNELIUS. No, no!

BARNABY. *(Crawling down stage of table and putting on shoes)* No, no!

MRS. MOLLOY. Minnie, this is the famous Cornelius Hackl, who goes round New York tying people into knots; and that's Barnaby Tucker, another trouble-maker.

BARNABY. How d'you do? *(Shoes on, he then rises to Left of table. Crosses up Left.)*

MRS. MOLLOY. *(Crossing down to her)* Minnie, choose yourself any hat and coat in the store. We're going out to dinner.

CORNELIUS. Pardon?

(MINNIE *to below table.* CORNELIUS *comes down to* MRS. MOLLOY. BARNABY *crosses up Left Centre.)*

MRS. MOLLOY. If this Mr. Hackl is so rich and gay and charming, he's going to be rich and gay and charming to us. He dines three times a week at the Harmonia Gardens Restaurant, does he? Well, he's taking us there now.

(CORNELIUS *has backed up stage again.*)

MINNIE. (*Crosses to counter.*) Mrs. Molloy, are you sure it's safe?

MRS. MOLLOY. Minnie, hold your tongue. We're in a position to put these men into jail if they so much as squeak.

CORNELIUS. Jail, Mrs. Molloy?

BARNABY. (*Crosses to* CORNELIUS.) Jail!

MRS. MOLLOY. (*Up to Right of him.*) Jail, Mr. Hackl. Officer Cogarty does everything I tell him to do.

(CORNELIUS *goes above table to* BARNABY.)
(MRS. MOLLOY *turns to* MINNIE.) Minnie, you and I have been respectable for years; now we're in disgrace, we might as well make the most of it.

(*They move to end of counter.*)
(*Takes her by shoulders.*) Come into the workroom with me; I know some ways we can perk up our appearance.

(CORNELIUS *and* BARNABY *cross up Left.* MINNIE *goes to workroom door.*)
(*Right up to* CORNELIUS.) Gentlemen, we'll be back in a minute. (*She goes towards workroom.*)

CORNELIUS. (*Crossing to counter*) Uh—Mrs. Molloy, I hear there's an awfully good restaurant at the railway station.

(BARNABY *crosses down Left Centre.*)

MRS. MOLLOY. Railway station? Railway station? Certainly not! No, sir! You're going to give us a good dinner in the heart of the fashionable world.

(*A squeak from* MINNIE.)
Go on in, Minnie! Don't you boys forget that you've made us lose our reputations, and now the fashionable

world's the only place we *can* eat. (*Exits to workroom; leaves door open.*)

BARNABY. She's angry at us, Cornelius. Maybe we'd better run away now. (*Crosses up Right below table to counter.*)

CORNELIUS. No, I'm going to go through with this if it kills me.

(*He brings gilt chair and sits facing* BARNABY, *who sits by the counter.*)

Barnaby, for a woman like that a man could consent to go back to Yonkers and be a success.

BARNABY. All I know is no woman's going to make a success out of me.

CORNELIUS. Jail or no jail, we're going to take those ladies out to dinner. So grit your teeth.

(MRS. MOLLOY *and* MINNIE *enter from workroom dressed for the street, but* MINNIE *has no hat.* MRS. MOLLOY *to below table to door.*)

MRS. MOLLOY. Gentlemen, the cabs are at the corner, so forward march! (*She takes hat for* MINNIE *from up stage leg of cheval mirror.*)

CORNELIUS. (*To above table.*) Yes, ma'am.

(BARNABY *stands shaking his empty pockets warningly.*)

Oh, Mrs. Molloy—is it far to the restaurant? Couldn't we walk?

MRS. MOLLOY. (*Pauses a moment, then:*) Minnie, take off your things. We're not going. (*Puts hat on table.*)

OTHERS. Mrs. Molloy!

(BARNABY *crosses down.*)

MRS. MOLLOY. Mr. Hackl, I don't go anywhere I'm not wanted. Good night. I'm not very happy to have met you. (*Crossing down stage to behind counter.*)

OTHERS. Mrs. Molloy!

MRS. MOLLOY. I suppose you think we're not fashionable enough for you?

CORNELIUS. No! No!

MRS. MOLLOY. Well, I won't be a burden to you. Good night, Mr. Tucker.

(The OTHERS *follow her behind counter:* CORNELIUS, BARNABY, *then* MINNIE.*)*

CORNELIUS. We want you to come with us more than anything in the world, Mrs. Molloy.

(MRS. MOLLOY *turns and pushes* CORNELIUS. *The* THREE *back out:* MINNIE *to top of counter,* BARNABY *below table,* CORNELIUS *below counter.)*

MRS. MOLLOY. No, you don't! Look at you! *(Moves around counter to* MINNIE.*)* Look at the pair of them, Minnie! Scowling, both of them!

CORNELIUS. Please, Mrs. Molloy!

MRS. MOLLOY. Then smile. *(To* BARNABY.*)* Go on, smile!

(BARNABY *hangs his head.)*

No, that's not enough. Minnie, you come with me and we'll get our own supper. *(Gives hat on table to* MINNIE *and* BOTH *go towards the door.)*

CORNELIUS. Smile, Barnaby, you lout!

BARNABY. My face can't smile any stronger than that.

MRS. MOLLOY. *(Coming back down to Left of table)* Then do something! Show some interest. Do something lively: sing!

CORNELIUS. *(Breaking up Right of table)* I can't sing, really I can't.

MRS. MOLLOY. We're wasting our time, Minnie. They don't want us.

CORNELIUS. Barnaby, what can you sing? Mrs. Molloy, all we know are sad songs.

MRS. MOLLOY. That doesn't matter. If you want us to come out with you, you've got to sing something.

(The Boys *turn up to counter, put their heads together, confer and abruptly turn, stand stiffly Right of table—*Barnaby *down Right,* Cornelius *up Right, and sing "Tenting tonight; tenting tonight; tenting on the old camp ground." The* Four *of them now repeat the refrain, softly, harmonising.)*

We'll come!

(The Boys *shout joyously.)*

You boys go ahead.

(Cornelius *gets his hat from counter; as he puts it on he discovers the flowers on it.* Barnaby *crosses below table and gets his hat from window.* Cornelius *puts flowers in pocket.* Minnie *turns and puts her hat on at the mirror.)*

Minnie, get the front door key—I'll lock the workroom. (Mrs. Molloy *to workroom.)*

(The Boys *go out, whistling.)*

Minnie. *(Takes key from hook, Left of wardrobe, and goes to* Mrs. Molloy. *She turns her round.)* Why, Mrs. Molloy, you're crying!

Mrs. Molloy. *(Flings her arms round* Minnie.) Oh, Minnie, the world is full of wonderful things. Watch me, dear, and tell me if my petticoat's showing. *(She crosses to door, followed by* Minnie, *as—*

THE CURTAIN FALLS

ACT THREE

*Verandah at the Harmonia Gardens Restaurant on the
Battery. The back of the set consists of three cloths.
The back cloth contains the two service doors —each
of two half-doors, painted green, and on swing hing-
es. Above these is painted "STAFF ONLY"—"IN"
—"OUT." Between these doors, pinned to the cloth,
is a large bamboo screen, which when pulled forward,
divides the room in half. The screen is in five folds,
and has a swing door in the Centre fold. In the two
down stage folds, small latticed grilles enable one
to see through. The second cloth contains two pillars
Right Centre and Left Centre and painted marble.
The sides of the cloth contain open arches. Between
this cloth and the third are inserted two archways,
running up and down-stage, and hung with beads.
These archways lead Right to the street and Left to
the upstairs rooms. The third, and down stage cloth,
contains one slender pillar, Centre, painted bamboo,
and at the sides, arches with low bamboo trellises at
the bottom. Down stage again is a wing each side,
painted bamboo trellis and leaves. From these wings,
a very low trellis of bamboo runs in a half-circle to
down Centre. A gap in the Centre allows an entrance, but this is used only by* MALACHI, COR-
NELIUS *and* BARNABY. *A cane table stands up Right
with three cane swivel chairs. A tall cane coat-tree
is up Right in front of marble pillar. Another stands
Left by the Left table. The screen is extended at
commencement.*

As the Curtain rises, VANDERGELDER *is standing down
Left giving orders to* RUDOLPH *up Right.* MALACHI
STACK *sits twisting round in chair Right of Left table.*

61

VANDERGELDER. Now, hear what I say. I don't want you to make any mistakes, I want a table for three.

RUDOLPH. For three.

VANDERGELDER. There'll be two ladies and myself.

MALACHI. It's a bad combination, Mr. Vandergelder. You'll regret it.

VANDERGELDER. And I want a chicken.

MALACHI. A chicken! You'll regret it.

VANDERGELDER. Hold your tongue. Write it down! Chicken.

RUDOLPH. Yes, sir. Chicken Esterhazy? Chicken Hunter style? Chicken à la crème?

VANDERGELDER. A chicken like everybody else has. And with the chicken I want a bottle of wine.

RUDOLPH. Moselle? Chablis? Beaujolais?

MALACHI. He doesn't understand English, Mr. Vandergelder. You'd better speak louder.

VANDERGELDER. (Spelling) W-I-N-E.

RUDOLPH. Vine.

VANDERGELDER. Vine! And I want this table removed. We'll eat at that table alone.

(RUDOLPH exits through Right service door.)

MALACHI. There are some people coming in here now, Mr. Vandergelder.

VANDERGELDER. (Goes up Right to look, then comes Centre again.) Oh, it's my niece and that artist— (Realizing, he turns up Right again.) Hey! What are they doing here? The traitors! The scoundrels!

MALACHI. (Running up to him) Mr. Vandergelder! Remember what Napoleon said.

VANDERGELDER. And there's Mrs. Levi, too. Let me get my hands on them.

MALACHI. Remember what Napoleon said, Mr. Vandergelder.

VANDERGELDER. Napoleon said what?

MALACHI. (Leading him down Left) First observe the enemy. Hide—listen. Hear what they're planning. Na-

poleon—be a Napoleon, sir. Outsmart them, Mr. Vandergelder.

(They hide behind the screen as MRS. LEVI, ERMENGARDE *and* AMBROSE *enter up Right. They pause by the Right table.* AMBROSE *is carrying the trunk and wicker case.)*

MRS. LEVI. Enjoy yourself, enjoy yourself. Now, Ermengarde, dear, there's nothing wicked about eating in a
restaurant. There's nothing wicked, even about being in
New York. Clergymen just make those things up to fill
out their sermons.

(They now cross to above Left table, AMBROSE *bringing the luggage.* VANDERGELDER *and* MALACHI *go through the door in the screen.* VANDERGELDER *to up Right.)*

ERMENGARDE. Oh, but I don't want to eat in a public
restaurant like this!
MRS. LEVI. That's all right, dear; there are some lovely
private rooms upstairs, just meant for shy, timid girls
like us.

(ERMENGARDE, MRS. LEVI *and* AMBROSE *exit up Left.)*

VANDERGELDER. *(Producing a pencil, crosses down; sits Right of Right table.)* Stack, I want to write a note.
MALACHI. *(Producing paper)* Oh, yes. Excuse me.
VANDERGELDER. Go and call that cabman in here. I
want to talk to him.
MALACHI. No one asks advice of a cabman, Mr. Van-
dergelder. They see so much of life that they have no ideas
left.
VANDERGELDER. Do as I tell you.
MALACHI. Yes, sir. Advice of a cabman! *(Exits through Right bead curtain.)*
VANDERGELDER. *(Writes his letter.)* "My dear Miss
Van Huysen"— *(To audience.)* Everybody's dear in a

letter. It's enough to make you give up writing 'em. "My dear Miss Van Huysen. This is Ermengarde and that rascal Ambrose Kemper. They are trying to run away.

(MALACHI *returns with an enormous* CABMAN *in a high hat and a long coat. He carries a whip.* MALACHI *crosses to Left table and sits down stage of it.*)

Keep them in your house until I come."

CABMAN. *(Entering)* What's he want?

VANDERGELDER. I want to talk to you.

CABMAN. *(Above table.)* I'm engaged. I'm waiting for my parties.

VANDERGELDER. *(Folding letter and writing address)* I know you are. Do you want to earn five dollars?

CABMAN. Eh?

VANDERGELDER. I asked you, do you want to earn five dollars?

CABMAN. I don't know. I never tried. *(Crosses Centre.)*

(VANDERGELDER *rises.* MALACHI *crosses down Left; sits in chair down of Left table.*)

VANDERGELDER. *(Rising, going round above table and crossing to Centre)* When those parties of yours come downstairs, I want you to drive them to this address. Never mind what they say, drive them to this address. Ring the bell! give this letter to the lady of the house! See that they get in the door and keep them there.

CABMAN. *(Letter in hand.)* I can't make people go into a house if they don't want to.

VANDERGELDER. *(Producing purse)* Can you for ten dollars?

CABMAN. Even for ten dollars, I can't do it alone.

VANDERGELDER. This fellow here will help you. *(He crosses Left.)*

(CABMAN *crosses Right.*)

MALACHI. *(To audience.)* Now I'm pushing people into houses.

VANDERGELDER. *(Reaching over and turning the address right way up)* There's the address! Miss Flora Van Huysen, eight Jackson Street.

CABMAN. Even if I get them in the door I can't be sure they'll stay there.

VANDERGELDER. *(Takes out another bill.)* For fifteen dollars you can.

MALACHI. *(To audience.)* Murder begins a twenty-five dollars.

VANDERGELDER. Hold your tongue! *(To* CABMAN.) The lady of the house will help you. All you have to do is to sit in the front hall and see that the man doesn't run off with the girl. *(Crosses up Right Centre.)* I'll be at Miss Van Huysen's in an hour or two and I'll pay you then. *(He goes above Right table.)*

CABMAN. *(Follows.)* If they call the police, I can't do anything.

(VANDERGELDER *crosses Centre.* CABMAN *crosses Centre.)*

VANDERGELDER. It's perfectly honest business. Perfectly honest. The young lady is my niece.

(CABMAN *laughs.)*
The young lady is my niece!!

CABMAN. Yes. *(Looks at* MALACHI *and shrugs.)*

VANDERGELDER. She's trying to run away with a good-for-nothing and we're preventing it.

CABMAN. Oh, I know them, sir. They'll win in the end. Rivers don't run up hill.

MALACHI. What did I tell you, Mr. Vandergelder? Advice of a cabman.

VANDERGELDER. *(Hits table with his stick.)* Stack!

(MALACHI *rises.)*
I'll be back in half an hour. See that the table's set for three. See that nobody else eats there. Then go and join the cabman on the box.

MALACHI. Very good, sir.

(VANDERGELDER *exits through bead curtain Right.)*

CABMAN. Who's your friend? *(Crosses Right Centre.)*

MALACHI. Friend!! That's not a friend; that's an employer I'm trying out for a few days. *(Sits down stage chair again. Produces the stub of a cigar.)*

CABMAN. You won't like him.

MALACHI. I can see you're in business for yourself because you talk about liking employers. No one's liked an employer since business began.

CABMAN. Aw—!

MALACHI. No, sir. I suppose you think *your horse* likes you?

CABMAN. My Old Clementine? She'd give her right feet for me. *(Little nearer to MALACHI.)*

MALACHI. That's what all employers think. You imagine it. The streets of New York are full of cabhorses winking at one another. *(Strikes match on sole of boot and lights cigar butt. Then rises, goes below CABMAN to up Right.)* Here, let's go in the kitchen and get some whiskey. I can't push people into houses when I'm sober. No, I've had about fifty employers in my life, but this is the most employer of them all. He talks to everybody as though he were paying them.

CABMAN. *(Going slowly round screen)* I had an employer once. He watched me from eight in the morning until six at night—just sat there and watched me. Oh, dear! *(Pokes his head through door in screen.)* Even my mother didn't think I was as interesting as all that. *(Exits through Left service door.)*

MALACHI. *(Following him off)* Yes, being employed is like being loved: You know that somebody is thinking about you the whole time. *(Exits.)*

(MRS. MOLLOY, MINNIE, BARNABY *and* CORNELIUS *enter through bead curtain Right.* MINNIE *goes to hang hat and coat on Left coat tree.* BARNABY *follows.* MRS. MOLLOY *laughs and enters on "I know.")*

MRS. MOLLOY. *(To down Centre.)* See! Here's the place I meant! Isn't it fine? Minnie, take off your things! We'll be here for hours.

CORNELIUS. *(Up Right.)* Mrs. Molloy, are you sure you'll like it here? I think I feel a draught.

MRS. MOLLOY. Indeed, I do like it. We're going to have a fine dinner right in this room; it's private, and it's elegant. Now we're all going to forget our troubles and call each other by our first names. *(Crosses back to him.)* Cornelius! *(Crossing Left again)* Call the waiter. *(Hangs her cloak Left.)*

CORNELIUS. Wai—Wai—I can't make a sound. I must have caught a cold on that ride. Wai—No! It won't come.

MRS. MOLLOY. I don't believe you. Barnaby, you call him.

BARNABY. *(Goes up Centre, through Left service door, out Right door and down.)* Waiter! Waiter!

(CORNELIUS *threatens him.* BARNABY *runs Left; hangs hat up.*)

MINNIE. *(Below table to down Centre.)* I never thought I'd be in such a place in my whole life. Mrs. Molloy, is this what they call a "café"?

MRS. MOLLOY. *(In up stage chair.)* Yes, this is a café. Sit down, Minnie. Cornelius, Mrs. Levi gave us to understand that every waiter in New York knew you.

CORNELIUS. *(Now down Centre.)* They will.

(MRS. MOLLOY *sits above table,* BARNABY *Left;* MINNIE *sits below.*)

RUDOLPH. *(Enters from Left service door. To Right of table.)* Good evening, ladies and gentlemen.

CORNELIUS. *(Shaking his hand)* How are you, Fritz? How are you, my friend?

RUDOLPH. I am Rudolph.

CORNELIUS. Of course. Rudolph, of course. Well, Rudolph, these ladies want a little something to eat—you know what I mean? Just if you can find the time—we know how busy you are.

MRS. MOLLOY. Cornelius, there's no need to be so familiar with the waiter. (*Takes menu from* RUDOLPH.)

CORNELIUS. Oh, yes, there is. (*Hands hat across table to* BARNABY, *who hangs it up.*)

MRS. MOLLOY. (*Passing menu across*) Minnie, what do you want to eat?

(RUDOLPH *closes the screen.*)

MINNIE. Just anything, Irene.

MRS. MOLLOY. No, speak up, Minnie. What do you want?

MINNIE. No, really, I have no appetite at all. (*Swings round in her chair and studies the menu.*)

(BOYS *watch her anxiously.*)

Oh— Oh— I'd like some sardines on toast and a glass of milk.

CORNELIUS. (*Takes menu from her.*) Great grindstones! What a sensible girl! Barnaby, shake Minnie's hands. She's the most sensible girl in the world. Rudolph, bring us gentlemen two glasses of beer, a loaf of bread and some cheese.

MRS. MOLLOY. (*Takes menu.*) I never heard of such nonsense. Cornelius, we've come here for a good dinner and a good time. Minnie, have you ever eaten pheasant?

MINNIE. Pheasant? No-o-o-o!

MRS. MOLLOY. Rudolph, have you any pheasant?

RUDOLPH. Yes, ma'am. Just in from New Jersey today.

MRS. MOLLOY. Even the pheasants are leaving New Jersey. (*She laughs loudly, pushing* CORNELIUS, *then* RUDOLPH.) Now, Rudolph, write this down: mock turtle soup; pheasant; mashed chestnuts; green salad; and some nice red wine. (*She does not read this from menu.*)

(RUDOLPH *repeats each item after her.*)

CORNELIUS. All right, Barnaby, you watch me. (*He reads from the bill of fare.*) Rudolph, write this down: Neapolitan ice-cream; hot-house peaches; champagne—

ALL. Champagne!

(BARNABY *spins round in his chair.*)

CORNELIUS. (*Holds up a finger.*) —and a German band. Have you got a German band?

MRS. MOLLOY. No, Cornelius, I won't let you be extravagant. Champagne, but no band. (*Rises and hands menu to* RUDOLPH.) Now, Rudolph, be quick about this. We're hungry.

RUDOLPH. Yes, ma'am. (*Exits.*)

MRS. MOLLOY. (*Hurries over up Right.*) Minnie, come upstairs. I have an idea about your hair. I think it'd be nice in two wee horns—

MINNIE. (*Hurrying after her, turns and looks at the* BOYS) Oh! Horns!

(*They go out. There is a long pause.* CORNELIUS *sits staring after them.* BARNABY *looks around in wonderment.*)

BARNABY. Cornelius, they say in the Army, you have to curry horses all the time.

CORNELIUS. (*Not turning*) Oh, that doesn't matter. By the time we get out of jail we can move right over to the Old Men's Home.

(*Another waiter,* AUGUST, *enters by Left service door bearing a bottle of champagne in cooler and five glasses.* MRS. MOLLOY *re-enters up Right and meets him down Centre.* MINNIE *follows to below her.*)

MRS. MOLLOY. Waiter! What's that? What's that you have?

AUGUST. It's some champagne, ma'am.

MRS. MOLLOY. Cornelius, it's our champagne.

(*They gather round* AUGUST, BARNABY *down stage,* CORNELIUS *Left.*)

AUGUST. No, no. It's for His Honour the Mayor of New York and he's very impatient.

MRS. MOLLOY. Shame on him! The Mayor of New York has more important things to be impatient about. Cornelius, open it.

(CORNELIUS *takes the bottle. The* OTHERS *take the glasses.*)

AUGUST. Ma'am, he'll kill me.
MRS. MOLLOY. Well, have a glass first and die happy.
AUGUST. (*Sits Right of Right table.*) He'll kill me.

(AUGUST *lays the cloth and napkins on Left table and starts off.*)

MRS. MOLLOY. I go to a public restaurant for the first time in ten years and all the waiters burst into tears. "He'll kill me!" There, take that and stop crying, love. (*She takes a glass to* AUGUST, *then comes back.*) Barnaby, make a toast!

(CORNELIUS *puts bottle on Left table.*)

BARNABY. (*Now Right of her.*) To all the ladies in the world—may I get to know more of them—and—may I get to know them better.
CORNELIUS. The ladies!
MRS. MOLLOY. That's *very* sweet and *very* refined. Minnie, for that I'm going to give Barnaby a kiss.
MINNIE. Oh! (*She runs across to below Left table, sits Left chair.*)
MRS. MOLLOY. Hold your tongue, Minnie. I'm old enough to be his mother, and— (*Indicating a height three feet from the floor*) A dear wee mother I would have been too. Barnaby, this is for you from all the ladies in the world. (*She kisses him.*)
BARNABY. (*At first dazed, then:*) Now I can go back to

Yonkers, Cornelius. Pudding. Pudding. Pudding! *(He spins round and falls on his knees.)*

MRS. MOLLOY. Look at Barnaby. He's not strong enough for a kiss. His head can't stand it.

(Exit AUGUST Right service door with tray and cooler. The sound of "The Skaters' Waltz" comes from off Left. CORNELIUS sits in chair at top of table. MINNIE is at Left, BARNABY Right and MRS. MOLLOY below. RUDOLPH enters to lay table, small plates, cruet and cutlery.)

Minnie, I'm enjoying myself. To think that this goes on in hundreds of places every night, while I sit at home darning my stockings.

(A GYPSY MUSICIAN appears from up Left playing a concertina. MRS. MOLLOY rises and dances away up Centre. THE GYPSY comes slowly round Right of table, pausing by MRS. MOLLOY, then slowly forward, concentrating on MINNIE. He goes right round the table and out of sight behind the Left marble pillar. The music softens.)

Cornelius, dance with me.

CORNELIUS. *(Rises; moves forward.)* Irene, the Hackls don't dance. We're Presbyterian.

(RUDOLPH exits with champagne glass.)

MRS. MOLLOY. Minnie, you dance with me.

(MINNIE joins her. CORNELIUS sits again. GYPSY reappears, playing, and comes Left of the GIRLS. The music is louder again.)

MINNIE. *(As he passes)* Lovely music.

(GYPSY continues down stage, round the GIRLS and up to Right bead curtain; makes eyes at them as they dance and exits.)

MRS. MOLLOY. Why, Minnie, you dance beautifully.

MINNIE. We girls dance in the work room when you're not looking, Irene.

MRS. MOLLOY. You thought I'd be cross and so you didn't ask me to dance.

(GIRLS *break and dance away*—MINNIE *to up Left behind balustrade,* MRS. MOLLOY *to Right table, where she sits in chair Right. The music softens again. There is a pause.*)

Cornelius! Jenny Lind and all those other ladies—do you see them all the time?

CORNELIUS. (*Rises, crosses and sits in Left chair.*) Irene, I've put them right out my head. I'm interested in—

(RUDOLPH *has entered by Right service door. He now throws tablecloth between them.* AUGUST *has followed* RUDOLPH *and now brings chair to below the table.*)

MRS. MOLLOY. Rudolph, what are you doing?

(CORNELIUS *rises; to above Left table.*)

RUDOLPH. A table's been reserved here. Special orders.

(MALACHI *gives loud laugh off stage.*)

MRS. MOLLOY. Stop right where you are. That party can eat inside. This verandah's ours.

RUDOLPH. I'm very sorry. This verandah is open to anybody who wants it. Ah, there comes the man who brought the order.

(MALACHI *enters from the kitchen, drunk, singing.*)

MRS. MOLLOY. (*To* MALACHI, *Centre.*) Take your table away from here. We got here first, Cornelius; throw him out.

MALACHI. Ma'am, my employer reserved this room at

four o'clock this afternoon. Youse ones can go and eat in the restaurant. My employer said it was very important that he have a table alone. *(He goes down Centre.)*

MRS. MOLLOY. *(Following him)* No, sir. We got here first and we're going to stay here—alone, too.

(AUGUST *to behind Right table with cutlery.* MINNIE *above Left table.* BARNABY *below it.* CORNELIUS *crosses behind* MRS. MOLLOY *to Right table.)*

RUDOLPH. Ladies and gentlemen! I have a suggestion.

MRS. MOLLOY. Shut up, you! *(To* MALACHI.*)* You're **an** impertinent, idiotic kill-joy.

MALACHI. *(Very pleased.)* That's an insult!

MRS. MOLLOY. All the facts about you are insults. *(To* CORNELIUS.*)* Cornelius, do something. Knock it over! The table.

CORNELIUS. Knock it over. *(He calmly overturns the table, then goes Centre, above* MRS. MOLLOY.*)*

(BARNABY *joins them.* ALL *laugh.* MALACHI *goes above Right table.* AUGUST *rights the table and picks up cutlery.* RUDOLPH *comes to down Centre, below* MRS. MOLLOY, CORNELIUS *and* BARNABY. GYPSY *enters.)*

RUDOLPH. I'm sorry, but this room can't be reserved for anyone. If you want to eat alone, you must go upstairs. I'm sorry, but that's the rule.

(CORNELIUS *blows in his face and goes to Right table again.)*

MRS. MOLLOY. We're having a nice dinner alone and we're going to stay here. Cornelius, knock it over.

(CORNELIUS *overturns the table again.* GIRLS *squeal with pleasure.* AUGUST. *again scrambles for the silver.* CORNELIUS *comes Centre, laughing as before.*

MALACHI *goes above Left table with the intention of overturning it.)*

MALACHI. Wait 'til you see my employer!

(From now on, ALL talk at the top of their voices. MRS. MOLLOY and MINNIE rush to save the table. CORNELIUS runs up to MALACHI and grasps him by the collar. The GYPSY enters. CORNELIUS rushes MALACHI out through the bead curtain Right. BARNABY follows. As they pass him, the GYPSY falls on his knees and crawls off through the Right service door. RUDOLPH now brings the screen down. CORNELIUS and BARNABY struggle to close the screen as RUDOLPH hangs on to it. MRS. MOLLOY stands on the chair Right of Left table. MINNIE stands on the chair above it. RUDOLPH attracts AUGUST to come and help him. AUGUST gets caught in the door as CORNELIUS and BARNABY succeed in closing the screen. AUGUST's arms wave wildly as he is pinned up against the cloth.)

RUDOLPH. *(Bringing screen down)* Ladies and gentlemen! I tell you what we'll do. We'll put the screen up between the tables.

MRS. MOLLOY. I won't eat behind a screen. I won't. Minnie, make a noise. We're not animals in a menagerie. Cornelius, no screen. Minnie, there's a fight. I feel ten years younger. No screen! No screen!

(As the screen is closed, RUDOLPH pulls CORNELIUS away above Left table, then goes to release AUGUST. MALACHI runs in from up Right, below BARNABY to Centre. BARNABY exits through bead curtain.)

MALACHI. *(Loud and clear.)* Now you'll learn something. There comes my employer now, getting out of that cab.

CORNELIUS. *(Coming to him, taking off his coat)* Where? I'll knock him down too.

(RUDOLPH comes down Centre, facing up stage. AUGUST follows him and goes below Right table. BARNABY returns to CORNELIUS. MALACHI goes above Right table.)

BARNABY. Cornelius, it's Wolf-Trap. Yes, it is!

CORNELIUS. Listen, everybody. I think the screen's a good idea. Have you got any more screens, Rudolph? We could do with three or four. *(He pulls the screen forward again.)*

MRS. MOLLOY. Quiet down, Cornelius, and stop changing your mind.

(BARNABY helps MRS. MOLLOY down from the chair and goes below table to above it. MINNIE gets down from her chair. She and BARNABY move the table a little up stage. AUGUST exits Right service door. RUDOLPH runs up stage. MRS. MOLLOY trips him, and he falls Left of screen.)

Hurry up, Rudolph, we're ready for the soup.

(RUDOLPH exits Left service door.)

(The stage is now divided in half. The quartet's table is at the Left. They arrange chairs round the table. Enter VANDERGELDER from the Right. Now wears overcoat and carries box of sweets.)

VANDERGELDER. Stack! What's the meaning of this? I told you I wanted a table alone. What's this? *(Hits the screen with his stick.)*

(MRS. MOLLOY hits back with a spoon. The FOUR sit: MRS. MOLLOY Right, MINNIE Left, CORNELIUS down stage, BARNABY up stage.)

MALACHI. Mr. Vandergelder, I did what I could. Mr.

Vandergelder, you wouldn't believe what wild savages the people of New York are. There's a woman over there, Mr. Vandergelder—civilization hasn't touched her.

VANDERGELDER. *(Sweets box on table. Hangs up hat and stick.)* Everything's wrong. You can't even manage a thing like that. Help me off with my coat. Don't kill me. Don't kill me. *(During the struggle with the overcoat,* VANDERGELDER'S *purse flies out of his pocket and falls by the screen.* VANDERGELDER *goes to the coat-tree and hangs his coat up.)*

MRS. MOLLOY. Speak up! I can't hear you.

CORNELIUS. My voice again. Barnaby, how's your throat? Can you speak?

BARNABY. Can't make a sound.

MRS. MOLLOY. Oh, all right. Bring your heads together, and we'll whisper.

VANDERGELDER. *(Sits Right of Right table.)* Who are those people over there?

MALACHI. Some city sparks and their girls, Mr. Vandergelder. What goes on in big cities, Mr. Vandergelder—best not think of it.

VANDERGELDER. Has that couple come down from upstairs yet? I hope they haven't gone off without your seeing them.

MALACHI. No, sir. Myself and the cabman have kept our eyes on everything.

VANDERGELDER. *(Gets paper from overcoat. Sits Right of Right table.)* I'll sit here and wait for my guests. You go out to the cab.

MALACHI. Yes, sir.

   *(*VANDERGELDER *unfurls newspaper and starts to read.)*

*(*MALACHI *sees the purse on the floor and picks it up.)* Eh? What's that? A purse. Did you drop something, Mr. Vandergelder?

VANDERGELDER. No. Don't bother me. Do as I tell you.

MALACHI. *(Coming Centre)* A purse. That fellow over there must have let it fall during the misunderstanding about the screen. No, I won't look inside. Twenty-dollar bills, dozens of them. I'll go over and give it to him. *(Starts toward* CORNELIUS, *then turns and says to audience:)* You're surprised? You're surprised to see me getting rid of this money so quickly, eh? I'll explain it to you.

*(*RUDOLPH *brings wine to Right of* CORNELIUS, *hands bottle, sets glasses, exits with soup plates.)*

There was a time in my life when my chief interest was picking up money that didn't belong to me. The law is there to protect property, but—sure, the law doesn't care whether a property owner deserves his property or not, and the law has to be corrected. There are several thousands of people in this country engaged in correcting the law. For a while, I, too, was engaged in the redistribution of superfluities.

*(*RUDOLPH *enters with meat plates.)*

A man works all his life and leaves a million to his widow. She sits in hotels and eats great meals and plays cards all afternoon and evening, with ten diamonds on her fingers. Call in the robbers! Call in the robbers! Or a man leaves it to his son who stands leaning against bars all night boring a bartender. Call in the robbers! Stealing's a weakness. There are some people who say you shouldn't have any weaknesses at all—no vices. But if a man has no vices, he's in great danger of making vices out of his virtues, and there's a spectacle. We've all seen them: men who were monsters of philanthropy and women who were dragons of purity. We've seen people who told the truth, though the Heavens fall,—and the Heavens fell. No, no—nurse one vice in your bosom. Give it the attention it deserves and let your virtues spring up modestly around it. Then you'll have the miser who's no liar; and the drunkard who's the benefactor of a whole city. Well, after I'd had that weakness of stealing for a while, I found another: I took to whisky—whisky took to me. And then I discovered an important rule that I'm going to pass on to you: Never support two weaknesses at the same time. It's your combination sinners—your lecherous liars and your miserly drunkards—who dishonor the vices and bring them into bad repute. So now you see why I want to get rid of this money: I want to keep my mind free to do the credit to whisky that it deserves. And my last word to you, ladies and gentlemen, ladies and gentlemen, is this: one vice at a time. *(Raises hat. Goes over to Right of* CORNELIUS.) Excuse me. Can I speak to you for a minute?

CORNELIUS. *(Rises.)* You certainly can. We all want to apologize to you about that screen—that little misunderstanding.

(They ALL rise, with exclamations of apology.)

MRS. MOLLOY. Yes, I'm very sorry.

MALACHI. Oh, it's nothing.

CORNELIUS. What's your name, sir?

MALACHI. Stack, sir. Malachi Stack. If you ladies will excuse me, I'd like to speak to you for a minute. *(Draws* CORNELIUS *down to down Centre.)*

(MRS. MOLLOY moves to below table Left, sits down stage. BARNABY *sits Right of it.)*

Listen, boy, have you lost—? Come here— *(Leads him down Centre.)* Have you lost something?

CORNELIUS. Mr. Stack, in this one day I've lost everything I own.

(RUDOLPH enters, serves ice-cream and takes the meat plates.)

MALACHI. There it is. *(Gives him purse.)* Don't mention it.

CORNELIUS. Why, Mr. Stack—you know what it is? It's a miracle.

MALACHI. Don't mention it.

CORNELIUS. Barnaby, come here a minute.

(BARNABY rises drunkenly. MALACHI *crosses below* CORNELIUS *to Left of him.)*

I want you to shake hands with Mr. Stack.

(BARNABY, napkin tucked into his collar, comes Right of CORNELIUS, *then below him to Centre.)*

Mr. Stack's just found the purse I lost, Barnaby. You know, the purse full of money. *(Shows him the purse.)*

BARNABY. *(Shaking his hand vigorously)* You're a wonderful man, Mr. Stack. *(Whilst shaking hands, he circles below* MALACHI.)

MALACHI. *(Backing away to Right of* CORNELIUS*)* Oh, it's nothing—nothing.

CORNELIUS. *(Now between them.)* I'm certainly glad I went to church all these years. You're a good person to know, Mr. Stack. In a way, Mr. Stack, where do you work?

MALACHI. Well, I've just begun. I work for a Mr. Vandergelder in Yonkers.

(CORNELIUS *is thunderstruck. He glances at* BARNABY *and turns to* MALACHI *with awe. All* THREE *are swaying slightly back and forth.)*

CORNELIUS. You do? It's a miracle. *(He points to the ceiling.)* Mr. Stack, I know you don't need it—

(MALACHI *now starts to move below* CORNELIUS *to Left whilst* BARNABY *circles below* MALACHI, *backwards, to Right of* CORNELIUS.)

but can I give you something for—for the good work?

MALACHI. *(Putting out his hand)* Don't mention it. It's nothing.

CORNELIUS. Take that. *(Hands him a note.)*

MALACHI. *(Taking note)* Don't mention it.

CORNELIUS. And that. *(Another note.)*

MALACHI. *(Takes it and moves away.)* I'd better be going.

(BARNABY *signals to give him another.*)

CORNELIUS. Oh, here. And that.

MALACHI. *(Hands third note back.)* No, I might get to like them. *(Exits down Left.)*

(CORNELIUS *bounds exultantly back to Left of table.*

BARNABY *goes Right of table and sits.* VANDERGELDER
returns newspaper to overcoat.)

CORNELIUS. Irene, I feel a lot better about everything.
(Gulps down a glass of wine.) Irene, I feel so well that
I'm going to tell the truth. *(Pulls chair down to* MRS.
MOLLOY.)

MRS. MOLLOY. I'd forgotten that, Minnie. Men get
drunk so differently from women. All right, what is the
truth?

CORNELIUS. If I tell the truth, will you let me—will you
let me put my arm around your waist?

(MINNIE screams and flings her napkin over her face.)

MRS. MOLLOY. Hold your tongue, Minnie. All right,
you can put your arm around my waist just to show it
can be done in a gentlemanly way. *(Turns her chair to
face Right.)* But I might as well warn you: A corset is
a corset.

CORNELIUS. *(His arm around her, softly)* You're a
wonderful person, Mrs. Molloy.

MRS. MOLLOY. Thank you. All right, now that's
enough. *(Turns to face him.)* What is the truth?

CORNELIUS. Irene, I'm not as rich as Mrs. Levi said I
was.

MRS. MOLLOY. Not rich!

CORNELIUS. I almost never came to New York. And
I'm not like she said I was—bad. And I think you ought
to know that at this very minute Mr. Vandergelder's
sitting on the other side of that screen.

MRS. MOLLOY. Well, now! He's not going to spoil any
party of mine. So that's why we've been whispering. Let's
forget all about Mr. Vandergelder and have some more
wine. *(She turns to the table and pours out wine, singing
loudly: "East Side, West Side, all around the town"—but
la-la's it instead of the words.)*

    *(*CORNELIUS *moves chair back in place.)*
Come on, you know the tune.

CORNELIUS. But I don't know the words.

(They ALL *join the second line: "The cops play Ring-o-Roses, London Bridge is falling down—" Their singing fades away on that.* MRS. LEVI *enters by the Right service door to* VANDERGELDER, *who rises, picks up sweets box.)*

MRS. LEVI. Good evening, Mr. Vandergelder. *(Shakes hands.)*

VANDERGELDER. Where's—where's Miss Simple?

MRS. LEVI. Mr. Vandergelder, I'll never trust a woman again as long as I live. *(Hangs up scarf and handbag.)*

VANDERGELDER. *(Crossing to Left of table)* Well? What is it?

MRS. LEVI. She ran away this afternoon and got married!

VANDERGELDER. She did?

MRS. LEVI. *(To Right of table, below* VANDERGELDER.) Married, Mr. Vandergelder, to a young boy of fifty.

VANDERGELDER. She did?

MRS. LEVI. Oh, I'm as disappointed as you are. *(Sits.)* I—can't—eat—a—thing—what—have—you—ordered?

VANDERGELDER. I ordered what you told me to, a chicken. *(Sits.)*

(Enter AUGUST *with cruet and napkins. He goes to* VANDERGELDER'S *table.)*

MRS. LEVI. I don't think I could face a chicken. Oh, waiter. How do you do? What's your name?

AUGUST. August, ma'am.

MRS. LEVI. August, this is Mr. Vandergelder of Yonkers—Yonkers' most influential citizen, in fact. I want you to see that he's served with the best you have and served promptly. And there'll only be the two of us. *(*MRS. LEVI *gives one set of cutlery to* AUGUST.)

*(*VANDERGELDER *puts candy box under table.)*

Mr. Vandergelder's been through some trying experi-

ences today—men hidden all over Mrs. Molloy's store—
like Indians in ambush.

VANDERGELDER. You don't have to tell him everything
about me.

*(The QUARTET commences singing very softly: "East
Side, West Side, all around the town. The cops play
Ring-o-Roses, London Bridge is falling down.")*

MRS. LEVI. Mr. Vandergelder, if you're thinking about
getting married, you might as well learn right now you
have to let women be women.
*(About this point, the QUARTET has reached the last
two lines of the song which they now sing very
loudly: "Boys and girls together, Me and Mamie
O'Rourke, Trip the light fantastic on the sidewalks
on New York," sustaining the note at the word "on.")*
Now, August, we want excellent service.

AUGUST. Yes, ma'am. *(Exits to kitchen.)*

VANDERGELDER. You've managed things very badly.
When I plan a thing it takes place.
(MRS. LEVI rises.)
Where are you going?

MRS. LEVI. Oh, I'd just like to see who's on the other
side of that screen. *(She goes through the door in the
screen.)*

*(AUGUST enters with a bottle of wine in cooler, which he
places on floor above table, and exits. As she appears,
the QUARTET falls silent.)*

CORNELIUS. *(Rising)* Good evening, Mrs. Levi.

*(MRS. LEVI takes no notice, but taking up the refrain
where they left off, she continues around the screen
and returns to her place at the Right table.)*

VANDERGELDER. Well, who was it?

MRS. LEVI. Oh, just some city sparks entertaining their girls, I guess.

VANDERGELDER. Always wanting to know everything; always curious about everything; always putting your nose into other people's affairs. Anybody who lived with you would get as nervous as a cat.

MRS. LEVI. What? What's that you're saying?

VANDERGELDER. I said anybody who lived with you would—

MRS. LEVI. Horace Vandergelder, get that idea right out of your head. I'm surprised that you even mentioned such a thing. Understand once and for all that I have no intention of marrying you.

VANDERGELDER. I didn't mean that.

(MRS. MOLLOY *rises, goes to screen and looks through down stage grille.*)

MRS. LEVI. You've been hinting around at such a thing for some time, but from now on put such ideas right out of your head.

VANDERGELDER. Stop talking that way. That's not what I meant at all.

MRS. LEVI. I hope not. I should hope not. Horace Vandergelder, you go your way— *(Points a finger.)* and I'll go mine. *(Points a finger in same direction.)* I'm not some Irene Molloy, whose head can be turned by a pot of geraniums.

(MRS. MOLLOY *turns and looks at* CORNELIUS.)
Why, the idea of you even suggesting such a thing.

VANDERGELDER. Mrs. Levi, you misunderstood me.

MRS. LEVI. I certainly hope I did. If I had any intention of marrying again it would be to a far more pleasure-loving man than you. Why, I'd marry Cornelius Hackl before I'd marry you.

(CORNELIUS *rises; places* MRS. MOLLOY'S *chair close by screen.* BARNABY *rises and goes above table.* CORNELIUS *takes a glass of wine, turns the Right chair round and sits on the back with feet on the seat. He*

and Mrs. Molloy *settle down to listen.* Barnaby *sits on floor above table and goes to sleep.* Minnie *turns away in her chair and eats ice-cream.)*
However, we won't discuss it any more.
    (Enter August *with a tray.)*
Here's August with our food! I'll serve it, August.
    August. Yes, ma'am. *(Sets the dishes, pours a taster of wine for* Vandergelder, *then hands bottle to him.)*
    Mrs. Levi. Here's some white meat for you, and some giblets, very tender and very good for you. No, as I said before, you go your way and I'll go mine.—Start right in on the wine. I think you'll feel better at once.
    (August exits.)
However, since you brought the matter up, there's one more thing I think I ought to say.
    Vandergelder. *(Rising in rage)* I didn't bring the matter up at all.
    Mrs. Levi. We'll have forgotten all about it in a moment, but—sit down,
        *(*Vandergelder *sits down.)*
sit down, we'll close the matter forever in just a moment, but there's one more thing I ought to say! It's true, I'm a woman who likes to know everything that's going on; who likes to manage things—you're right about that. But I wouldn't like to manage anything as disorderly as your household, as out-of-control, as untidy. You'll have to do that yourself, God helping you. *(Takes a mouthful of food and mumbles the last three words.)*
    Vandergelder. It's not out-of-control.
    Mrs. Levi. Very well, let's not say another word about it. Take some more of that squash; it's good. No, Horace, a complaining, quarrelsome, friendless soul like you is no sort of companion for me. *(Picks up pepper pot.)* You go your way— *(Peppers her own plate.)* and I'll go mine. *(Peppers his plate.)*
    Vandergelder. Stop saying that.
    Mrs. Levi. I won't say another word.
    Vandergelder. Besides— I'm not those things you said I am.

MRS. LEVI. What?—Well, I guess you're friendless, aren't you? Ermengarde told me this morning you'd even quarreled with your barber—a man who's held a razor to your throat for twenty years! Seems to me that that's sinking pretty low. *(Eats.)*

VANDERGELDER. Well, we had a little discussion and I said—but—my clerks, they—

MRS. LEVI. They like you? Cornelius Hackl and that Barnaby? Behind your back they call you Wolf-Trap.

(CORNELIUS *gets down from chair, puts glass on table, then sits in chair again, a little nearer* MRS. MOLLOY. BARNABY *comes and kneels up stage of him, whilst* MINNIE *bends across chairback between them.)*

VANDERGELDER. *(Blanching)* They don't.

MRS. LEVI. No, Horace. It looks to me as though I were the last person in the world that liked you, and even I'm just so-so. No, for the rest of my life I intend to enjoy myself. You'll be able to find some housekeeper who can prepare you three meals for a dollar a day—it can be done if you like cold baked beans. You'll spend your last days listening at keyholes, for fear someone's cheating you. Take some more of that. *(Offers a dish.)*

VANDERGELDER. Dolly, you're a damned exasperating woman.

MRS. LEVI. There! You see? That's the difference between us. I'd be nagging you all day to get some spirit into you. You could be a perfectly charming, witty, amiable man if you wanted to.

VANDERGELDER. *(Rising)* I don't want to be charming.

MRS. LEVI. But you are. Look at you now. You can't hide it. *(Eats.)*

VANDERGELDER. Listening at keyholes! Dolly, you have no right to say such things to me.

MRS. LEVI. At your age you ought to enjoy hearing the honest truth. You and I are too old to be talking nonsense to one another. *(Eats.)*

VANDERGELDER. My age! My age! You're always talking about my age.

MRS. LEVI. I don't know what your age is, but I do know that up at Yonkers with bad food and bad temper you'll double it in six months.

(VANDERGELDER *sits.*)

Let's talk of something else; but before we leave the subject there's one more thing I *am* going to say.

VANDERGELDER. Don't!

MRS. LEVI. Sometimes, just sometimes, I think I'd be tempted to marry you out of sheer pity; and if the confusion in your house gets any worse I may *have* to.

VANDERGELDER. I haven't asked you to marry me.

MRS. LEVI. Well, please don't. (*Eats.*)

VANDERGELDER. And my house is not in confusion.

MRS. LEVI. What? With your niece upstairs in the restaurant right now?

VANDERGELDER. I've fixed that better than you know.

MRS. LEVI. And your clerks skipping around New York behind your back?

VANDERGELDER. They're in Yonkers where they always are.

MRS. LEVI. Nonsense!

VANDERGELDER. What do you mean, nonsense?

MRS. LEVI. Cornelius Hackl's the other side of that screen this very minute.

VANDERGELDER. It ain't the same man!

MRS. LEVI. All right. Go on. Push it, knock it down. Go and see. (*Eats.*)

(VANDERGELDER *rises and goes towards the screen. The* FOUR *rise, agitated.* CORNELIUS *holds down stage fold, whilst* MRS. MOLLY *braces him from behind.* MINNIE *holds the screen door.* BARNABY *barricades the door with the table.*)

VANDERGELDER. (*Sitting again*) I don't believe it.

MRS. LEVI. All right. All right. Eat your chicken. Of course, Horace, if your affairs went from bad to worse and you became actually miserable, I might feel that it was my duty to come up to Yonkers and be of some assistance to you. After all, I was your wife's oldest friend.

VANDERGELDER. I don't know how you ever got any such notion. Now understand, once and for all, I have no intention of marrying *anybody*. Now, I'm tired and I don't want to talk.

(CORNELIUS *turns away to Left, seeing a way of escape.*)

MRS. LEVI. I won't say another word, either. *(Continues to eat.)*

CORNELIUS. Irene, I think we'd better go.
(MRS. MOLLOY *comes to him. He offers her the purse.*)
You take this money and pay the bill. Oh, don't worry, it's not mine.

MRS. MOLLOY. *(Crossing below to Left of him)* No, no, I'll tell you what we'll do. You boys put on our coats and veils.
(MINNIE *comes down to Right of* CORNELIUS.)
And if he comes stamping over here, he'll think you're girls.

CORNELIUS. What! Those things!

MRS. MOLLOY. Yes. Come on.

(She and MINNIE *take the clothes from the Left stand, and all* FOUR *exit up Left, using the exit above the bead curtain.)*

VANDERGELDER. *(Rises.)* I've got a headache. I've had a bad day. I'm going to Flora Van Huysen's, and then I'm going back to my hotel. *(Reaches for his purse.)* So, here's the money to pay for the dinner. *(Searching another pocket.)* Here's the money to pay for the— *(Going through all his pockets)* Here's the money— I've lost my purse!!

MRS. LEVI. Impossible! I can't imagine you without your purse.

VANDERGELDER. It's been stolen. (*Searching overcoat.*) Or I left it in the cab. What am I going to do? I'm new at the hotel!! They don't know me. (*Comes to Left of table.*) I've never been here before— Stop eating the chicken; I can't pay for it!

MRS. LEVI. (*Laughs.*) Horace, I'll be able to find some money. Sit down and calm yourself.

VANDERGELDER. Dolly Gallagher, I gave you twenty-five dollars this morning.

(CORNELIUS *returns to Left Center wearing* MRS. MOLLOY'S *cape. He counts the money in the purse.*)

MRS. LEVI. I haven't a cent. I gave it to my lawyer. We can borrow it from Ambrose Kemper, upstairs.

VANDERGELDER. I wouldn't take it. (*He looks in the wine cooler, and puts it on the table. Also puts sweets box on table.*)

MRS. LEVI. (*Rises. Sees* CORNELIUS.) Cornelius Hackl will lend it to us.

VANDERGELDER. He's in Yonkers. (*He moves her chair to Right, moves table over to it and looks on the floor.*)

(MRS. LEVI *stands Right of table and continues to eat.*)

MRS. MOLLOY. (*Returns and comes Left of* CORNELIUS.) Cornelius, is that Mr. Vandergelder's purse?

CORNELIUS. I didn't know it myself. I thought it was money just wandering around loose that didn't belong to anybody.

MRS. MOLLOY. Goodness! That's what politicians think!

(*Loud, wild gypsy MUSIC now starts, and from here to the end of the Act, everything goes at tremendous pace.*)

VANDERGELDER. Waiter! Waiter!

(AUGUST *enters with two plates of jelly on a tray. He uses Right service door. Simultaneously,* VANDERGELDER *goes through Left half of same door.* AUGUST *quickly puts plates on table.* VANDERGELDER *comes back, and* AUGUST *runs off again, throwing up a napkin as he goes.* VANDERGELDER *pauses to catch this, then follows* AUGUST. *Off-stage,* AUGUST *shouts "Rudolph!" and a CRASH of cutlery is heard.* GYPSY *now enters up Right. He clears to Centre as* VANDERGELDER *comes back and searches the floor below Right table.* RUDOLPH *crosses at back to assist* AUGUST. *On the Left of the screen,* MINNIE *brings* BARNABY *in dressed in her hat and coat.*)

MINNIE. Irene, doesn't Barnaby make a lovely girl? He just ought to stay that way.

MRS. MOLLOY. There's that gypsy again. Why should we have our evening spoiled? Cornelius, I can teach you to dance in a few minutes. Oh, he won't recognize you.

MINNIE. Barnaby, it's the easiest thing in the world.

(MRS. MOLLOY *and* BARNABY *move the table up stage.* MINNIE *and* CORNELIUS *move two chairs over to Left. The other two chairs remain close to the screen. They now form a circle, waiting for a cue in the music. The* GYPSY *is down Centre. On* VANDERGELDER'S *re-entrance,* MRS. LEVI *has moved over to Right Centre.* VANDERGELDER *moves the third chair down stage, still looking for his purse.* RUDOLPH *is seen looking over Right service door.*)

MRS. LEVI. Listen to that music. Horace, you danced with me at your wedding and you danced with me at mine. Do you remember?

VANDERGELDER. (*Moves below her, still looking.*) No. Yes.

MRS. LEVI. Horace, you were a good dancer then. Don't confess to me that you're too old to dance.

VANDERGELDER. I'm not too old. I just don't want to dance.

(At this point EVERYBODY *begins to dance:* VANDER-GELDER *and* MRS. LEVI, *too.)*

MRS. LEVI. Listen to that music.

(On the Left, BARNABY *and* MINNIE *break up stage together, whilst* MRS. MOLLOY *and* CORNELIUS *dance down stage by screen,* CORNELIUS *facing Left. The* GYPSY *makes a circle from Center to Left, round above* BARNABY *and* MINNIE, *and comes down between them as they raise their arms.* MRS. LEVI *and* VANDERGELDER *cross each other twice, then* VAN-DERGELDER, *with right hand on his own chair, and facing Right, shoots out his left leg Russian style, calling "Hey! Hey! Hey!" On the third call,* COR-NELIUS, *dancing backwards, falls over* VANDERGEL-DER'S *leg. For a moment they look at each other, then with a loud exclamation,* VANDERGELDER *recognizes him.* CORNELIUS *rises, rushes over Left and collapses into the down stage chair.* MINNIE, *with a scream, and* MRS. MOLLOY, *run in front of him as* VANDER-GELDER *comes rushing over. The* GYPSY *exits up Left.* BARNABY *hides behind the Left pillar.* MRS. LEVI *sits in chair down Right, laughing.* RUDOLPH *now crosses at back and looks over Left service door.)*

VANDERGELDER. You're discharged! Not a word! You're fired! Where's that idiot, Barnaby Tucker? *(He runs up and round the pillar.)*
(As he does so, CORNELIUS *goes to front of pillar.* ERMENGARDE *enters up Left, followed by* AMBROSE *with the two pieces of luggage, which he puts down immediately he is through the bead curtain.* MINNIE *moves to Centre and* BARNABY *runs down between her and* MRS. MOLLOY. CORNELIUS *runs through the screen door and is the first of the four to exit up Right, followed by* BARNABY, MINNIE *and* MRS. MOLLOY. RUDOLPH *picks up* MRS. MOLLOY'S *bag from Left table and hands it to her through screen*

door as she comes up on the other side. AUGUST *enters by Left service door with* VANDERGELDER'S *bill on a plate. He takes* CORNELIUS'S *place in front of Left pillar and stands writing the bill.* VANDERGELDER, *chasing* BARNABY, *meets* ERMENGARDE *and shakes a fist at her. She faints.* AMBROSE *catches her as she falls.* VANDERGELDER *turns and runs through the screen, making for his hat and coat.* AMBROSE, *carrying* ERMENGARDE, *exits by Left service door. He continues round through Right service door and exits through up Right bead curtain after the* QUARTET. VANDERGELDER *is through the screen in time to call after the* QUARTET:)

You're discharged!

MRS. MOLLOY. *(As she exits)* You're discharged!

VANDERGELDER. You're discharged!

(AUGUST *has followed* VANDERGELDER *through the screen and stands close to Right of it whilst* VANDERGELDER *takes his clothes from the stand and sweets box from table.* RUDOLPH, *as soon as* AMBROSE *is clear, picks up the luggage, runs below the screen and puts it down off Right, using the exit below the bead curtain.* VANDERGELDER *is on his way round below the screen as* MRS. LEVI *runs behind him, through the screen, in time to face him Left.)*

MRS. LEVI. Mr. Vandergelder, there's your life, without niece, without clerks—

(RUDOLPH *runs from Right through the screen after* MRS. LEVI. AUGUST *is just below the screen.* VANDERGELDER *now runs through the screen once more,* MRS. LEVI *following, and* AUGUST *following her. At the same time,* RUDOLPH *makes a wide circle down stage to Right.)*

—without bride, without purse. Will you marry me now?

VANDERGELDER. *(Continuing round screen)* NO!

MRS. LEVI. *(Now down Centre. To audience:)* DAMN!

(VANDERGELDER *runs out through the Left service door.* AUGUST *follows him.* RUDOLPH *goes quickly through the screen again; follows them.* MRS. LEVI *flounces round and through the screen to Right as the—*

CURTAIN FALLS

ACT FOUR

Miss Flora Van Huysen's house.

*The back cloth contains double doors. Cloth painted pic-
tures each side of doors. A backing to the doors is
painted: pictures, clock, barometer, etc. A second
cloth contains a large opening, Centre, painted with
curtains. Right of opening, painted pictures. Left is
painted with a small pipe organ. Left again, a painted
window with lace curtains. The Left wing is built as
a truck, carrying an upholstered window seat and
painted window and lace curtains. From the wing
hang four wicker bird cages, each draped with col-
oured shawl. The Right wing is painted with a china
cabinet and a draped curtain. Through the Centre
doors the street is to the Left and the kitchen is to
the Right. A double-ended sofa stands Right. An
aspidistra behind it, an upholstered diabolo stool in
front. Down Centre is a large upholstered pouffe. Left
is a single-ended sofa covered with a bright woolen
spread. It has five cushions on it. Close to Right of
sofa is a narrow table with a plant and several china
ornaments. An arm chair stands down Left, below
the window seat. Outside the Centre doors is an
upholstered ottoman.*

(Miss Van Huysen *is lying on the Left sofa. The* Cook
*is above window seat, where the gap between wing
and cloth gives the impression of the open window.*
Miss Van Huysen, *50, florid, stout and sentimental,
is taking snuff.* Cook *(enormous) has a china mixing
bowl beside her on window seat.*)

Cook. *(Coming to Left of sofa with bowl)* No, ma'am,
I could swear I heard a cab drawing up to the door.

MISS VAN HUYSEN. You imagined it. Imagination. Everything in life—like that—disappointment—illusion. Our plans—our hope— What becomes of them? Nothing. The story of my life. *(Sings to herself a minute.)*

COOK. *(Stirs. To window and back.)* Pray God nothing's happened to the dear girl. Is it long journey from Yonkers?

MISS VAN HUYSEN. No; but long enough for a thousand things to happen.

COOK. *(Crossing below pouffe to above it)* Well, we've been waiting all day. Don't you think we ought to call the police about it?

MISS VAN HUYSEN. The police! If it's God's will, the police can't prevent it. Oh, in three days, in a week, in a year, we'll know what's happened— And if anything really terrible *has* happened to Ermengarde, it'll be a lesson to him that's what it'll be.

COOK. To who?

MISS VAN HUYSEN. To that cruel uncle of hers, of course—to Horace Vandergelder, and to everyone else who tries to separate young lovers. Young lovers have enough to contend with as it is. Who should know that better that I? No one. The story of my life.

(She hums for a moment, COOK stirring in time with her.)

There! Now I hear a cab. Quick! *(Takes smelling salts from table.)*

COOK. *(Crosses up stage to window.)* No. No, ma'am. I don't see anything.

MISS VAN HUYSEN. There! What did I tell you? Everything's imagination—illusion. *(Snuffs the smelling salts.)*

COOK. *(To above sofa to Centre, sits on pouffe, mixing cake in bowl.)* But surely, if they've changed their plans, Mr. Vandergelder would have sent you a message.

MISS VAN HUYSEN. Oh, I know what's the matter. That poor child probably thought she was coming to another prison—to another tyrant. If she'd known that I was her friend, and a friend of all young lovers, she'd be here by now. *(Starts searching for her smelling salts amongst the ornaments on the table beside her.)* Oh yes, she would. Her life shall not be crossed with obstacles and disappointments as— Cook, a minute ago my smelling salts were on this table, now they completely disappeared. *(She puts her feet down and begins to throw the five cushions, one by one, on the floor.)*

(Cook puts bowl on table, kneels by the sofa and picks them up, putting each one on the foot of the sofa whilst Miss Van Huysen returns them to the head of the sofa. The last one she bangs on Cook's head as she kneels forward to look for the bottle. Cook puts last cushion on sofa and sits back.)

Cook. Why, there they are, ma'am, right there in your hand.

Miss Van Huysen. Goodness! How did they get there? *(Raises a finger.)* I won't inquire. Stranger things have happened. *(She hums a few notes of Handel's "Largo.")*

Cook. *(Gets her bowl and sits on foot of sofa.)* I suppose Mr. Vandergelder was sending her down with someone?

Miss Van Huysen. *(Sniffing salts)* Two can go astray as easily as— *(She sneezes.)*

Cook. God bless you! *(Runs above sofa to window.)* Now, here's a carriage stopping.

(The DOORBELL rings.)

Miss Van Huysen. *(Sniffing salts)* Well, open the door, Cook.
   (Cook exits to hall.)
It's probably— *(Sneezes again.)* God bless you.
   (SOUNDS of an altercation off Left.)
It almost sounds as though I heard voices.

Cornelius. *(Off.)* I don't want to come in. This is a free country, I tell you.

Cabman. *(Off.)* Forward march!

MALACHI. *(Off.)* In you go. We have orders.

CORNELIUS. *(Off.)* You can't make a person go where he doesn't want to go.

(Enter MALACHI, *who comes below the sofa table, followed by* COOK, *who remains up Right. The* CABMAN *bundles* BARNABY *and* CORNELIUS *into the room. They fight their way—out again.)*

MALACHI. Begging your pardon, ma'am, are you Miss Van Huysen?

MISS VAN HUYSEN. Yes, I am unfortunately. What's all this noise about?

(The NOISE stops off-stage. COOK *goes into the hall, stands Right.)*

*(*MALACHI *comes back down stage.)* There are two people here that Mr. Vandergelder said must be brought to this house and kept here until he comes. And here's his letter to you. *(He hands the note and collapses on foot of sofa, facing Centre.)*

MISS VAN HUYSEN. No one has any right to tell me whom I'm to keep in my house if they don't want to stay. *(She slaps* MALACHI *on the back.)*

MALACHI. *(Slaps* MISS VAN HUYSEN *on thigh.)* You're right, ma'am. Everybody's always talking about people breaking into houses, ma'am; but there are more people in the world who want to break out of houses that's what I always say— Bring them in, Joe.

(Enter CORNELIUS *and* BARNABY *being pushed by the* CABMAN. BARNABY *is still wearing* MINNIE'S *hat and coat and veil.* BARNABY *to pouffe, arguing with* COOK. CORNELIUS *comes down to sofa table; takes his hat off and puts it on table.)*

CORNELIUS. This young lady and I have no business here. We jumped into a cab and asked to be driven to the station and these men brought us to the house and forced us to come inside. There's been a mistake.

CABMAN. *(Comes below* CORNELIUS, *leans over table.)*
Is your name Miss Van Huysen?

MISS VAN HUYSEN. *(Rising and going to head of sofa)*
Everybody's asking me if my name's Miss Van Huysen. I
think that's a matter I can decide for myself. Now will
you all be quiet while I read this letter—

> (BARNABY *sits Left side of pouffe.* CORNELIUS *crosses
> below it and sits on Right side.* CABMAN *works
> round Centre and sits down stage end of Right sofa.*
> COOK *sits in chair at doors.* MISS VAN HUYSEN *comes
> round above Left sofa reading:)*

"This is *Ermengarde* and that rascal Ambrose Kemper"—
(To BARNABY.) Now I know who you *two* are, anyway.
(Reads.) "They are trying to run away—" *(Laughs.)*
Story of my life. *(Now goes above pouffe to Right of it.)*
Mr. Kemper, you have nothing to fear. *(To* CABMAN.)
Who are you?

CABMAN. I'm Joe. I stay here until the old man comes.
He owes me fifteen dollars.

MALACHI. *(Arranging himself full length on the sofa)*
That's right, Miss Van Huysen, we must stay here to see
they don't escape. *(Removes hat—puts it on his chest
with hands folded over it.)*

MISS VAN HUYSEN. *(To* BARNABY.) My dear child,
take off your things. We'll all have some coffee. *(To*
MALACHI *and* CABMAN.) You two go out and wait in the
hall. I'll send coffee out to you. Cook, take them.

> (COOK *goes down to* CABMAN, *gets him on his feet, then
> goes above Left of sofa to* MALACHI. MISS VAN
> HUYSEN *moves to Left of pouffe.* BARNABY *remains
> seated.* CORNELIUS *rises to above them.)*

CORNELIUS. Ma'am, we're not the people you're expecting, and there's no reason—

MISS VAN HUYSEN. Mr. Kemper, I'm not the tyrant
you think I am—

> (CORNELIUS *and* BARNABY *try to interrupt her.)*

You don't have to be afraid of me—

(They try to interrupt again.)
I know you're trying to run away with this innocent girl.

(MALACHI *is now on his feet and is arguing with* COOK.
MISS VAN HUYSEN *turns to them.)*

MALACHI. Dicky bird!
MISS VAN HUYSEN. Oh, get along.
   (COOK *shepherds* MALACHI *and* CABMAN *into the
   hall, where they sit on the ottoman—*CABMAN *on the
   Right. Presently* MALACHI *produces a flask which
   they share.* COOK *returns to up Right.)*
(To the BOYS.) All my life I have suffered from the inter-
ference of others. But you shall not suffer as I did. So
put yourself entirely in my hands. *(She lifts* BARNABY'S
veil.) Ermengarde! *(Kisses him on both cheeks.)* Where's
your luggage?
   BARNABY. It's—uh—uh—it's—
   CORNELIUS. Oh, I'll find it in the morning. It's been
mislaid.
   MISS VAN HUYSEN. Mislaid! How like life! Well,
Ermengarde; you shall put on some of my clothes.
   BARNABY. Oh, I know I wouldn't be happy really.
*(Rises and goes down Right. Walks backwards into
diabolo stool. Sits on it and rises again.)*
   MISS VAN HUYSEN. She's a shy little thing, isn't she?
Timid little darling!—Cook!
   COOK. *(Steps down.)* Yes, ma'am.
   MISS VAN HUYSEN. Go and put some gingerbread in
the oven and get the coffee ready—
   COOK. Yes, ma'am. *(Exits to kitchen.)*
   MISS VAN HUYSEN. —while I go and draw a good hot
bath for Ermengarde.

(BARNABY *runs up to Right of her.)*

   CORNELIUS. Oh, oh—Miss Van Huysen—
   MISS VAN HUYSEN. Believe me, Ermengarde, your

troubles are at an end. You two will be married tomorrow.

(CORNELIUS, *overcome, crosses down stage to window.*)

(*To* BARNABY, *hand under his chin.*) My dear, you look just like I did at your age, and your sufferings have been as mine. While you're bathing I'll come and tell you the story of my life.

BARNABY. (*Crossing below her to sofa table*) Oh, I don't want to take a bath. I always catch cold.

MISS VAN HUYSEN. No, dear, you won't catch cold. I'll slap you all over. I'll be back in a minute. (*She exits to kitchen.*)

CORNELIUS. (*Looking out of window*) Barnaby, do you think we could jump down from this window?

BARNABY. (*Above sofa to him.*) Yes—we'd kill ourselves. (*He continues on, below sofa and pouffe up to doorway.*)

CORNELIUS. (*Sits on window seat.*) We'll just have to stay here and watch for something to happen. Barnaby, the situation's desperate.

BARNABY. (*Coming down from door*) It began getting desperate about half-past four and it's been getting worse ever since. Now I have to take a bath and get slapped all over.

MISS VAN HUYSEN. (*Enters from kitchen. Claps her hands.*) Ermengarde—

(BARNABY *rises, rushes wildly below sofa to* CORNELIUS, *who seizes him and pushes him above sofa over to Centre.* BARNABY *passes above* MISS VAN HUYSEN *to Right of her.*)

— you've still got those wet things on. Your bath's nearly ready.

(*Turns to* CORNELIUS, *who has come Left of her.* BARNABY *sits.*)

Mr. Kemper, you come into the kitchen and put your feet in the oven.

(*The DOORBELL rings.*)

(Dramatically to CORNELIUS.) What's that? It's the doorbell. *(Turns to* BARNABY.) I expect it's your uncle.

(CORNELIUS *goes to window.* COOK *enters from kitchen.*)

COOK. There's the doorbell. *(Above sofa to window and looks out, above* CORNELIUS.)
      (MISS VAN HUYSEN *to window, behind her.* BAR-NABY *runs below sofa to window.*)
It's *another* man and a girl in a cab!
      MISS VAN HUYSEN. *(Pulling her away)* Well, go and let them in, Cook.
      (COOK *exits to front door.*)
(MISS VAN HUYSEN *seizes* BARNABY *and pushes him above sofa in front of her, then takes* CORNELIUS *by the hand, dragging him along.*) Now you two come with me.

*(She takes them out to the kitchen—*BARNABY *protesting, in front,* CORNELIUS *being dragged backward, still looking towards the window. There are SOUNDS of argument from front door.*)

BARNABY. But I don't want to take a bath. I had one on Saturday!
      COOK. *(Off.)* No, that's impossible. Come in, anyway.
      (Enter ERMENGARDE *to above sofa table.* AMBROSE, *carrying trunk and suitcase, goes to Right sofa and sits on up stage end. Removes hat.)*
(COOK *follows to up Centre.*) There's some mistake. I'll tell Miss Van Huysen, but there's some mistake.
      ERMENGARDE. But, I tell you, I *am* Mr. Vandergelder's niece; I'm Ermengarde.
      COOK. Beg your pardon, Miss, but you *can't* be Miss Ermengarde.
      ERMENGARDE. But—but—here I *am.* And that's my baggage.
      COOK. *(Bobbing to* AMBROSE) How do you do? *(To* ERMENGARDE.) I'll tell Miss Van Huysen who you *think* you are, she won't like it. *(Exits to kitchen.)*

AMBROSE. *(Rises to Centre.)* You'll be all right now, Ermengarde. I'd better go before she sees me.

ERMENGARDE. Oh, no. You must stay. I feel so strange here.

AMBROSE. I know, but Mr. Vandergelder will be here in a minute—

ERMENGARDE. Ambrose, you can't go—

MALACHI *and* CABMAN. *(From the hall.)* Ambrose, you can't go. *(They laugh.)*

(AMBROSE *and* ERMENGARDE *cross Left; sit on window-seat.)*

ERMENGARDE. You can't leave me in this crazy house with these drunken men in the hall.

(AMBROSE *crosses back Centre; peeks; crosses down Left Centre.)*

Ambrose— *(Crosses down Left of* AMBROSE.) Ambrose, let's say you're someone else that my uncle sent down to take care of me. Let's say you're—you're Cornelius Hackl!

AMBROSE. Who's Cornelius Hackl?

ERMENGARDE. You know. He's chief clerk in Uncle's store.

AMBROSE. I don't want to be Cornelius Hackl. *(Crossing below sofa to Right, putting hat on)* No, no, Ermengarde, come away with me now. *(Picks up trunk.)* I'll take you to my friend's house. Or I'll take you to Mrs. Levi's house. *(Picks up case, and moves Centre.)*

(As he picks up luggage, MALACHI *and* CABMAN *come into the doorway and stand with folded arms, barring the way.* ERMENGARDE *runs above and to Right of* AMBROSE, *pushing him over above sofa.)*

ERMENGARDE. Why, it was Mrs. Levi who threw us right at Uncle Horace's face.

(AMBROSE *puts trunk down close to window seat and the case on the seat.)*

(ERMINGARDE *comes and sits on foot of Left sofa.)* Oh, I

wish I were back in Yonkers where nothing ever happens.

MISS VAN HUYSEN. *(Enters between* MALACHI *and* CABMAN *to up stage.)* What's all this I hear? I told you to wait in the hall. Who do you say you are?

(AMBROSE *removes hat.)*

ERMENGARDE. *(Goes to Left of* MISS VAN HUYSEN.) Aunt Flora—don't you remember me? I'm Ermengarde.

(MALACHI *and* CABMAN *go back to hall.)*

MISS VAN HUYSEN. And you're Mr. Vandergelder's niece?

ERMENGARDE. Yes, I am.

MISS VAN HUYSEN. But, he has just sent me another niece named Ermengarde.

ERMENGARDE. But he doesn't—

MISS VAN HUYSEN. —And who is this?

ERMENGARDE. This is Cornelius Hackl, Aunt Flora.

MISS VAN HUYSEN. Never heard of him.

(AMBROSE *puts hat on window seat.)*

ERMENGARDE. He's chief clerk in Uncle's store.

MISS VAN HUYSEN. Never heard of him. The other Ermengarde came with the man she's in love with, and that *proves* it. *(Crosses below* ERMENGARDE *to sofa table. Addresses* AMBROSE.) She came with Mr. Ambrose Kemper.

AMBROSE *and* ERMENGARDE. *(Shout.)* Ambrose Kemper!

MISS VAN HUYSEN. Yes, Mr. Hackl, and Mr. Ambrose Kemper—

(ERMENGARDE *starts to cry.* AMBROSE *turns, throws hat on window seat.* MISS VAN HUYSEN *takes her to the sofa Left and they both sit,* ERMENGARDE *down stage.)*

Dear child, what is your trouble?

ERMENGARDE. Oh, dear. Nobody's anybody any more!

MISS VAN HUYSEN. *(In a low voice.)* Are you in love with this man?

ERMENGARDE. Yes, I am.

MISS VAN HUYSEN. I could see it—and are people trying to separate you?

ERMENGARDE. Yes, they are.

MISS VAN HUYSEN. I could see it—who? Horace Vandergelder?

ERMENGARDE. Yes.

MISS VAN HUYSEN. *(Draws AMBROSE down to sit on her other side; shakes his hand.)* Mr. Hackl, think of me as your friend. Now, we'll all go into the kitchen and get warm— *(She rises, goes Left of pouffe to up stage.)*

   They follow—ERMENGARDE going Right of pouffe and AMBROSE Left of it.)

(Turns.) We can decide later who everybody is. My dear, would you like a good hot bath?

ERMENGARDE. Yes, I would.

MISS VAN HUYSEN. Well, when Ermengarde comes out you can go in.

CORNELIUS. *(Enters from the kitchen.)* Oh, Miss Van Huysen—

ERMENGARDE. Why, Mr. Hack—!!

CORNELIUS. *(Sliding up to her urgently)* Not yet! I'll explain—I'll explain everything. *(He mouths these words silently.)*

(CORNELIUS drives ERMENGARDE down Right until she falls over the diabolo stool and sits on it.)

MISS VAN HUYSEN. Mr. Kemper! Mr. Kemper!

   (CORNELIUS turns.)

This is Cornelius Hackl.

   (CORNELIUS to Right of MISS VAN HUYSEN, AMBROSE Left of her.)

Mr. Hackl, this is Mr. Ambrose Kemper. Perhaps you two know one another.

AMBROSE. No! No!

CORNELIUS. No, we don't.

AMBROSE. *(Going above sofa to Left)* Miss Van Huysen, I know that man is not Ambrose Kemper.

CORNELIUS. And he's not Cornelius Hackl.

MISS VAN HUYSEN. *(To above sofa table.)* My dear young man, what does it matter what your names are? The important thing is that you are you. *(To AMBROSE.)* You are alive and breathing, aren't you, Mr. Hackl? *(Pinches AMBROSE's arm.)*

AMBROSE. Ouch, Miss Van Huysen.

MISS VAN HUYSEN. *(Below sofa and Left of pouffee to up Centre.)* This dear child imagines she is Horace Vandergelder's niece, Ermengarde.

ERMINGARDE. But I am.

MISS VAN HUYSEN. The important thing is that you're all in love. Everything else is illusion. *(Moves to CORNELIUS and pinches his Right arm.)*

CORNELIUS. Ouch! Miss Van Huysen!

MISS VAN HUYSEN. *(Comes down Left of pouffe to address the audience.)* Everybody keeps asking me if I'm Miss Van Huy— *(She breaks off, pinches her own arm, smiles in relief, then turns to face up stage.)* Now, you two gentlemen sit down and have a nice chat while this dear child has a good hot bath.

(ERMENGARDE crosses to MISS VAN HUYSEN. CORNELIUS runs above them and below sofa to window. He passes behind AMBROSE, who joins him at the window. MISS VAN HUYSEN and ERMENGARDE, Left hand in Left hand, run Left of pouffe to doorway. As they reach it, the COOK runs in from kitchen. MISS VAN HUYSEN and ERMINGARDE, still holding hands, circle round each other, bringing them on opposite sides, and COOK ducks under their raised hands. DOORBELL.)

COOK. There's the doorbell again.

MISS VAN HUYSEN. *(Now Right of her.)* Well, answer it.

(She and ERMENGARDE *exit to kitchen.* COOK *continues her run, below sofa to window, and looks out with the* BOYS.*)*

COOK. It's a cab and three ladies. *(Comes down stage rubbing her hands.)* I never saw such a night. Ha, ha! *(Gives a little skip and runs below sofa to door.)*

*(*MISS VAN HUYSEN *comes back, also rubbing her hands. As they pass, they both give a little skip. As* COOK *exits to front door,* MALACHI *and* CABMAN *make a grab for her, and both fall off the ottoman. They sit on the floor.* MISS VAN HUYSEN *goes above sofa table. The* BOYS *turn from the window—*AMBROSE *above* CORNELIUS.*)*

MISS VAN HUYSEN. Gentlemen, you can rest easy. *(Crossing over to Right sofa, fussing with cushions)* I'll see that Mr. Vandergelder lets his nieces marry you both.

(Enter MRS. LEVI. *She has to step over* MALACHI'S *legs. She goes over to* MISS VAN HUYSEN.*)*

MRS. LEVI. Flora, how are you? *(Kiss.)*
MISS VAN HUYSEN. Dolly Gallagher! What brings you here?

(They sit on Right sofa.)

MRS. LEVI. Great Heavens, Flora, what are those two drunken men doing in your hall?
MISS VAN HUYSEN. I don't know. Horace Vandergelder sent them to me.
MRS. LEVI. *(Rises.)* Well, I've brought you two girls in much the same condition. Otherwise they're the finest girls in the world.
(She goes up to the door and leads in MRS. MOLLOY. MINNIE *follows.* CORNELIUS *steps close to sofa.* AMBROSE *passes down stage behind him.)*

I want you to meet Irene Molloy.

MISS VAN HUYSEN. Delighted to know you.

(They shake hands. MRS. MOLLOY sits, unsteadily, on Left side of pouffe.)

MRS. LEVI. And this is Minnie Fay.

(She passes MINNIE across to MISS VAN HUYSEN, who carefully sits her on the diabolo stool down Right. COOK off to kitchen. MINNIE is almost in a trance-like state and sits on the stool, facing up stage and swaying gently. MRS. LEVI turns up Centre and sees CORNELIUS and AMBROSE.)

Oh, I see you two gentlemen are here, too. Mr. Hackl, I was about to look for you *somewhere* here.

CORNELIUS. No, Mrs. Levi. I'm ready to face anything now.

MRS. LEVI. Mr. Vandergelder will be here in a minute. He's downstairs trying to pay for a cab without any money.

MRS. MOLLOY. Oh, I'll help him. *(She has VANDERGELDER'S purse and has been fumbling in her own handbag. Now she rises, holding her bag upside down and spilling the contents. MRS. MOLLOY sits again.)*

(CORNELIUS runs below pouffe, AMBROSE on his Left, MISS VAN 'IUYSEN on his Right. ALL kneel and pick up the dollar bills, etc., from the floor.)

MRS. LEVI. *(Coming down to her)* Yes, will you, dear? You had to pay the restaurant bills. You must have hundreds of dollars there it seems.

MRS. MOLLOY. This is his own purse he lost. I can't give it back to him without seeming—

(VANDERGELDER'S voice is heard out in the hall, in argument with another CABMAN. CORNELIUS runs down to window, followed by AMBROSE. MISS VAN HUYSEN runs down to window.)

MRS. LEVI. I'll give it back to him—there, you help him with this now. *(She gives* MRS. MOLLOY *a bill and keeps the purse. She goes up behind Right sofa.)*

MRS. MOLLOY. *(Exits to front door. Off.)* I'll take care of that, Mr. Vandergelder.

(As VANDERGELDER *enters,* MALACHI *and the* CABMAN *rise and follow him in.* VANDERGELDER *carries overcoat, stick and sweets box.)*

MALACHI. Hello, Mr. Vandergelder. How are you?

CABMAN. *(Right.)* Fifteen dollars, Mr. Vandergelder.

VANDERGELDER. *(To* MALACHI.) You're discharged! *(To* CABMAN.) You too! *(Goes down, passing Right of pouffe.)*

*(*MALACHI *and* CABMAN *exit, sit in hall again. This time* MALACHI *is Right.)*

So I've caught up with you at last! *(Crosses below pouffe to foot of Left sofa. To* AMBROSE.) I never want to see you again! *(To* CORNELIUS.) You're discharged! Get out of the house, both of you. *(He strikes sofa with his stick.)*

*(*MISS VAN HUYSEN *comes to above* VANDERGELDER *and hits him with a newspaper. He turns.)*

MISS VAN HUYSEN. Now then you. Stop ordering people out of my house. You can shout and carry on in Yonkers—

*(*VANDERGELDER *crosses to Right.)*

—but when you're in my house you'll behave yourself.

VANDERGELDER. They're both dishonest scoundrels.

MISS VAN HUYSEN. Take your hat off.

(He does so.)

Gentlemen, you stay right where you are.

CORNELIUS. *(Starts to cross below sofa.)* Mr. Vandergelder, I can explain— *(He slips and collapses on foot of sofa.)*

MISS VAN HUYSEN. *(Stroking his hair)* There aren't

going to be any explanations. Horace, stop scowling at Mr. Kemper and forgive him.

VANDERGELDER. That's not Kemper, that's a dishonest rogue named Cornelius Hackl.

MISS VAN HUYSEN. You're crazy. *(Points to* AMBROSE.) That's Cornelius Hackl.

VANDERGELDER. I guess I know my own chief clerk.

MISS VAN HUYSEN. I don't care what their names are. You shake hands with them both, or out you go.

VANDERGELDER. *(Sits Right side of pouffe.)* Shake hands with those dogs and scoundrels!

MRS. LEVI. *(To Right of* VANDERGELDER.) Mr. Vandergelder, you've had a hard day. You don't want to go out in the rain now. Just for *form's* sake, shake hands with them. You can start quarrelling again tomorrow. *(She returns to behind the sofa.)*

*(*CORNELIUS *rises.)*

VANDERGELDER. *(Crosses below him—then, turning, gives* CORNELIUS *one finger to shake.)* There! Don't regard that as a handshake.
    (He turns to AMBROSE, *who offers him one finger.)*
Hey! I never want to see you again. (VANDERGELDER *goes above Left sofa.)*

*(*MINNIE *falls off stool.* CORNELIUS *and* AMBROSE *go to pick her up.)*

MINNIE. Don't push.

*(*CORNELIUS *is above and* AMBROSE *below her.)*

MRS. MOLLOY. *(Enters from front door.)* Miss Van Huysen.

MISS VAN HUYSEN. *(Is above* CORNELIUS.) Yes, dear?

MRS. MOLLOY. Do I smell coffee?

MISS VAN HUYSEN. *(Up Centre to her.)* Yes, dear.

MRS. MOLLOY. Can I have some, good and black?

(MINNIE *rises and starts to waltz, trance-like, across below Left sofa.*)

MISS VAN HUYSEN. Come along, everybody. We'll all go into the kitchen and have some coffee.
(CORNELIUS *joins* MRS. MOLLOY *and exits with her to kitchen.* MALACHI *and* CABMAN *follow.* AMBROSE *follows them.* MISS VAN HUYSEN *takes* VANDER- GELDER *out.*)
(As they go.) Horace, you'll be interested to know there are two Ermengardes in there—

(MINNIE *continues her waltz round the Left sofa and out to the kitchen.* MRS. LEVI, *left alone, comes to front of Right sofa, addressing an imaginary Eph- raim down Right.*)

MRS. LEVI. Ephraim Levi, I'm going to get married again. Ephraim, I'm marrying Horace Vandergelder for his money. I'm going to send his money out doing all the things you taught me. Oh, it won't be a marriage in the sense that we had one—but I shall certainly make him happy, and—Ephraim—I'm tired. I'm tired of living from hand to mouth, and I'm asking your permission, Ephraim—will you give me away? *(Now addressing the audience she holds up the purse, crosses to below pouffe and sits.)* Money, money, money—it's like the sun we walk under: it can kill and it can cure. Horace Vander- gelder's never tired of saying most of the people in the world are fools, and in a way he's right, isn't he? Himself, Irene, Cornelius, myself! But there comes a moment in everybody's life when he must decide whether he'll live among human beings or not—a fool among fools or a fool alone. As for me, I've decided to live among them. *(Crosses and sits down Right end of sofa L.)* I wasn't always so. After my husband's death I retired into my- self. Yes, in the evenings, I'd put out the cat and I'd lock the door and make myself a little rum toddy; and before I went to bed I'd say a little prayer thanking God that I was independent—that no one else's life was mixed up with mine. And when ten o'clock sounded from Trinity Church Tower I fell off to sleep and I was a perfectly contented woman. And one night, after two years of this, an oak leaf fell out of my Bible. I had placed it there on the day my husband asked me to marry him: a perfectly good oak leaf—but without color and without life. And suddenly—I realized that for a long time I had not shed one tear; nor had I been for one moment outrageously happy; nor had I been filled with the wonderful hope that something or other would turn out well. I saw that I was like that oak leaf and on that night I decided to rejoin the human race. On that night I heard many hours struck off from Trinity Church Tower. You and I have known lots of people who've decided—like Horace Vandergelder —like myself for a long time—not to live among human beings. Yes, they move out among them, they talk to them, they even get married to them; but at heart they have decided not to have anything to do with the human race. If you accept human beings and are willing to live among them you acknowledge that every man has a right to his own mistakes. *(Rises to down Centre.)* Yes, we're all fools and we're all in danger of creating a good deal of havoc in the world with our folly; but the one way to keep us from harm is to fill our lives with the four or five human pleasures which are our right in the world; *and that takes a little money.* Not much, but a little. The difference between a little money and no money at all is enormous and can shatter the world; and the difference between a little money and an enormous amount of money is very slight and that, also, can shatter the world. Money —pardon my expression—money is like manure; it's not worth a thing unless it's spread around encouraging young things to grow. *(Sits on pouffe Centre.)* Anyway, that's the opinion of the second Mrs. Horace Vandergelder.

VANDERGELDER. *(Enters up Centre with two cups of coffee. With his back, he closes both doors. Coming Left of her)* Miss Van Huysen asked me to bring you this.

MRS. LEVI. Thank you both. Sit down and rest yourself.

VANDERGELDER. No thank you. I'm not tired.

MRS. LEVI. What's been going on in the kitchen?

VANDERGELDER. *(Below sofa, facing up stage.)* A lot of foolishness. Everybody's falling in love with everybody. I forgave 'em; Ermengarde and that artist.

MRS. LEVI. I knew you would—two? *(Holding up sugar from her saucer.)*

VANDERGELDER. Thank you. *(Takes sugar from her.)* I made Cornelius Hackl my partner.

MRS. LEVI. You won't regret it.

VANDERGELDER. *(Sits Left side of pouffe.)* Dolly, you said some mighty unpleasant things to me in the restaurant tonight—all that about my house—and everything.

MRS. LEVI. Let's not say another word about it.

VANDERGELDER. Dolly, you have a lot of faults.

MRS. LEVI. Oh, I know what you mean.

VANDERGELDER. You're bossy, you're scheming, you're inquisitive— You're—a—

MRS. LEVI. *(Turning away)* Go on.

VANDERGELDER. *(Rises; crosses to sofa table; turns.)* But you're—you're a wonderful woman. Dolly, marry me.

MRS. LEVI. Horace! *(Rises; to Right of pouffe.)* Stop right there.

VANDERGELDER. I know I've been a fool about Mrs. Molloy, and that other woman. But, Dolly, forgive me and marry me. *(He goes on his knees.)*

MRS. LEVI. *(Puts her cup on the pouffe.)* Horace, I don't dare. No. I don't dare.

VANDERGELDER. What do you mean?

MRS. LEVI. You know as well as I do that you're the first citizen of Yonkers. Naturally, you'd expect your wife to keep open house, to have scores of friends in and out all the time. Any wife of yours should be used to that kind of thing.

VANDERGELDER. Dolly, you can live any way you like.

MRS. LEVI. Horace, you can't deny it, your wife would

have to be a *somebody*. Answer me! Am I a somebody?

VANDERGELDER. You are—you are. Wonderful woman.

MRS. LEVI. Oh, you're partial. *(She crosses below pouffe and sits on foot of Left sofa facing Right.)*

(VANDERGELDER follows on his knees to her.)

Horace, it won't be enough for you to load your wife with money.

(He rises hastily, puts cup on table as he goes up stage.)

and jewels; to insist that she be a benefactress to half the town.

(He goes round sofa, coughing loudly.)

Horace, do you really think I have it in me to be a credit to you?

VANDERGELDER. *(Left of sofa.)* Dolly, everybody knows that you could do anything you wanted to do.

MRS. LEVI. I'll try. With your help, I'll try—and by the way, I found your purse. *(Holds it up.)*

VANDERGELDER. Where did you—? Wonderful woman!

MRS. LEVI. It just walked into my hand. I don't know how I do it. Sometimes I frighten myself. Horace, take it. Money walks out of my hands, too.

VANDERGELDER. Keep it. Keep it.

MRS. LEVI. *(Overcome, she turns away.)* Horace— I never thought—I'd ever— *(Turns to him with open arms.)* hear you say a thing like that!

(One knee on sofa, VANDERGELDER embraces her. BAR-NABY dashes in from the kitchen in great excitement to Centre. He is in his own clothes again.)

BARNABY. Oh! Excuse me. I didn't know anybody was here.

VANDERGELDER. *(Bellowing)* Didn't know anybody was here. Idiot!

(BARNABY moves to go.)

MRS. LEVI. *(Putting her hand on VANDERGELDER's arm; amiably)* Come in, Barnaby. Come in.

VANDERGELDER. *(Looks at her a minute, then says, imitating her tone:)* Come in, Barnaby. Come in.

BARNABY. *(Comes back.)* Cornelius is going to marry Mrs. Molloy.

MRS. LEVI. Isn't that fine! Horace—! *(Rises to face VANDERGELDER.)*

VANDERGELDER. *(Rises.)* Barnaby, go in and tell the rest of them that Mrs. Levi has consented—

MRS. LEVI. *(Turns to BARNABY.)* *Finally* consented!

VANDERGELDER. Finally consented to become my wife.

BARNABY. Holy cabooses! *(Dashes back to the doorway.)* Hey! Listen, everybody! Wolf-Trap—I mean— Mr. Vandergelder is going to marry Mrs. Levi. *(Goes to front of Right sofa.)*

(MISS VAN HUYSEN enters, followed by ALL the people in this Act. She is now carrying the sweets box.)

MISS VAN HUYSEN. Dolly, that's the best news I ever heard. *(She addresses the audience.)* There isn't any more coffee; there isn't any more gingerbread; but there are three couples in my house and they're all going to get married. And do you know, one of those Ermengardes wasn't a dear little girl at all—she was a boy! Well, that's what life is: disappointment, illusion.

MRS. LEVI. *(To audience.)* There isn't any more coffee; there isn't any more gingerbread, and there isn't any more play—but there is one more thing that we have to do— Barnaby, come here. *(She whispers to him, pointing to the audience. Then she says to the audience:)* I think the youngest person here ought to tell us what the moral of the play is.

(BARNABY is reluctantly pushed forward to footlights.)

BARNABY. Oh, I think it's about— I think it's about adventure. The test of an adventure is that when you're in the middle of it, you say to yourself, "Oh, now I've got myself into an awful mess; I wish I were sitting quietly at home." And the sign that something's wrong with you is when you sit quietly at home wishing you were out having lots of adventures. So that now we all want to thank you for coming tonight, and we all hope that in your lives you have just the right amount of sitting quietly at home, and just the right amount of . . . adventure. Goodnight!

THE CURTAIN FALLS

THE MATCHMAKER

PROPERTY PLOT

ACT ONE

By Window R.
 Pile of boxes
 Pieces of canvas
 Lengths of rope
 Rat trap
Tables D.R.
 Loaf of bread and knife on board
 Piece of cheese on enamel plate
 Coffee pot and enamel mug
 Chairs R. and L. of tables
Under L. Table
 4 bundles of newspapers
Above Archway R.
 Box
 Sack
On Flat above Tables R.
 Monkey stick with kettles, pans, dustpans and ladles
Desk up L.
 Shaving brush and mug
 Razor and strap
 2 towels
 Soft brush, comb and scissors
 2 account books
 Papers
 Inkstand with three quill pens
 Letter rack with luggage labels and pencil
On Floor above Desk
 Copper water can, stewpans, frying pans, black
  kettle

On Floor R. of Desk
Small Gladstone bag
Hand mirror
Large Gladstone bag
On chair below desk
Barber's cape
On Second Wing L.
Monkey stick with copper water can, kettles, stew-
pans, dustpans and brushes
Shelf with pots, coil of rope, pieces of harness
On Floor by Second Wing L.
Dustbin on board
Coil of rope
Folded carpet and pieces of red carpet
Feather broom and bits of canvas
Off up C.
Vandergelder's sword, sash and banner
Off L.
Basket trunk
Small basket

PERSONALS

MRS. LEVI
Handbag with two visiting cards
Parcel
VANDERGELDER
Purse
Watch
MALACHI STACK
Letters of recommendation.

ACT TWO

Second Wing R.
2 piles hatboxes
Third Wing R.
Pile of hatboxes
On Counter R.
Blue striped hatbox

Grey tulle hat with green box
Red velvet hat
Straw hat with cherries
Black straw hat with pink roses
Under Counter
Bonnet with blue ribbons
Straw hat with yellow roses
Straw hat with tall flowers
Grey velvet hat with bird
Grey and black tulle hat
On Stage of Counter
Milliner's chair upstage end
Milliner's chair D.S. end with gingham hat
Cupboard up C.
8 coats
Cuphook on L. end with key on ring
Centre Stage
Circular rug
Table C.
Red velvet cover
Tray of trimmings
Hat with butterfly
2 pieces of veiling
Bunch of violets with pin
Pincushion
Chair up C.
Cerise striped hatbox with Italian straw hat and
ribbon bow
Bonnet on top of box
Down L.
Profile hats
Piece of veiling
2 striped hatboxes

PERSONALS

VANDERGELDER
Cane
Hat
Box of chocolates

Mrs. Molloy
   Overslippers
   Handbag
Barnaby
   Coins

ACT THREE

Second Wing D.R.
   Cane chair
Stage R.
   Square cane table
   2 cane chairs
Below Pillar R.
   Hatstand
Stage L.
   Square cane table
   4 revolving chairs
Below Rostrum L.
   Hatstand
Off up L.
   Tray with: 4 plates of pheasant, lettuce
   Tray with: 4 soup plates, 4 side plates, 4 icecream
      plates, cruet, 4 wine glasses
Off up L.
   Tray with: 4 dinner knives, 4 dessert knives, 4 din-
      ner forks, 4 dessert forks, 4 soup spoons, 4
      dessert spoons, 4 teaspoons
   Bottle of red wine
   Menu
   2 tablecloths and 4 napkins
   Napkin for waiter
   Bill block and pencil
Off up R.
   Tray with: 3 plates, dish of sliced banana with table-
      spoon and fork, dish of pears with tablespoon
      and fork, 2 wine glasses
   Tray with: 5 champagne glasses, bottle of cham-
      pagne in cooler

Tray with: 3 dinner knives, 6 forks, 3 dessert spoons,
   2 soup spoons, 3 dessert knives, cruet
3 napkins
Bottle of white wine in cooler
Bill block and pencil

Off R.

Corded trunk
Basket trunk
Box of chocolates

PERSONALS

VANDERGELDER
Purse
Newspaper
Pencil
MALACHI STACK
Cigars
Matches
Purse

ACT FOUR

First Wing D.R.
Gilt potstand with rose china bowl and fern
Upstage R. Wing
4-fold screen
Right
Sofa with three floral cushions, antimacassar on D.S.
   arm
Diabolo pouffe
Centre Stage
Blue pouffe
R. of C. door
Lacquered chair
L. of C. door
Brass potstand with pot of leaves
Table C.
Runner
Blue vase

Blue dish with smelling **salts**
Heartshaped workbox
Snuffbox
Pinbox
Bowl with green leaves
Blue and white bowl with lid
Sofa L.C.
5 cushions
Crocheted cover
Below Organ up L.
Green upholstered stool
Footrest
Window seat
Upholstered seat
3 small cushions
Newspaper
Upstage of Window
Bird cage with plaid cover
Bird cage with purple cover
C. of Window
Bird cage with black embroidered cover
Large bird cage with pink floral cover
D.S. of Window
Red upholstered chair
Bird cage with purple cover on stand
In hall
Upholstered seat
Off L.
Corded trunk
Basket trunk
Mixing bowl and spoon
Off R.
2 cups of coffee with lump of sugar in each saucer

PERSONALS

MALACHI STACK
Letter
Whiskey flask

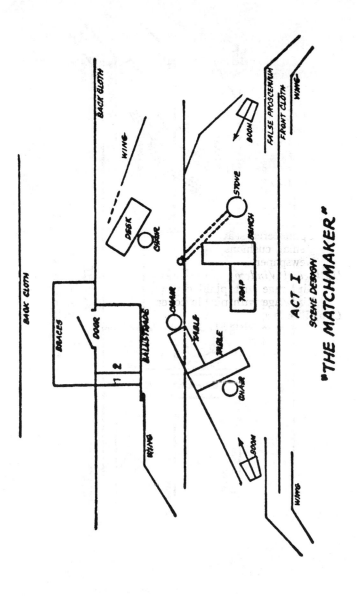

ACT I

SCENE DESIGN

"THE MATCHMAKER"

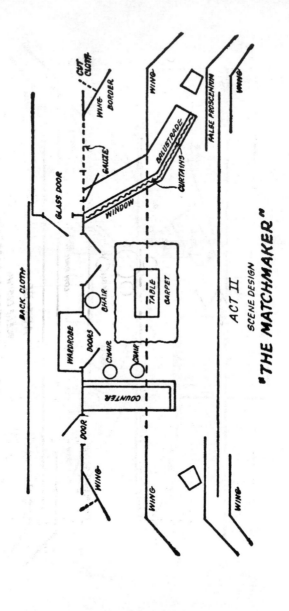

ACT II

SCENE DESIGN

"THE MATCHMAKER"

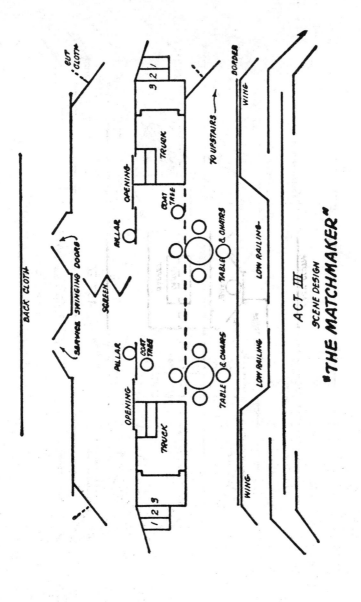

ACT III
SCENE DESIGN
"THE MATCHMAKER"

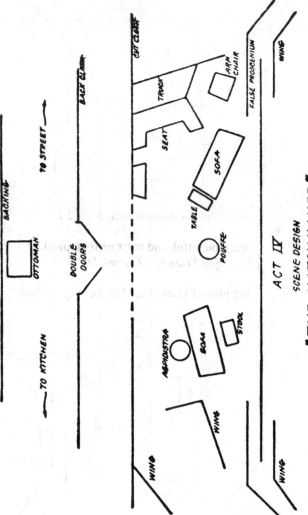

ACT IV

SCENE DESIGN

"THE MATCHMAKER"

The Twilight of the Golds

a comic drama by

Jonathan Tolins

If your parents knew everything about your before you were born, would you be here? That is the question posed in this entertaining drama. All is well when Suzanne Gold and her close New York family discover that she is pregnant, until a new prenatal test reveals that the baby will most likely be homosexual. 3 m., 2 f.

"Funny, thoughtful, and most eerily topical."
San Francisco Chronicle

"A haunting play of ideas crucial to the way we live."
Rex Reed

"An entertaining theatrical tempest."
Washington Times

"A rich, intelligent, articulate piece of work that speaks volumes to matters that are paramount to us today."
Los Angeles Times

GREAT PLAYWRIGHTS, GREAT PLAYS

James Goldman	THE LION IN WINTER
Robert Bolt	A MAN FOR ALL SEASONS
Neil Simon	PROPOSALS
Alan Ayckbourn	COMMUNICATING DOORS
Samuel Beckett	ENDGAME
Bertolt Brecht	MOTHER COURAGE AND HER CHILDREN
Agatha Christie	THE MOUSETRAP
Noel Coward	BLITHE SPIRIT
Georges Feydeau	A FLEA IN HER EAR
Eugene Ionesco	THE BALD SOPRANO
David Mamet	THE OLD NEIGHBORHOOD
Christopher Hampton	LES LIAISONS DANGEREUSES
Dario Fo	WE WON'T PAY! WE WON'T PAY!
Athol Fugard	VALLEY SONG
George Bernard Shaw	MISALLIANCE
Thornton Wilder	OUR TOWN

These are among the thousands of plays in Samuel French's
BASIC CATALOG OF PLAYS AND MUSICALS

Samuel French, Inc.
THE HOUSE OF PLAYS SINCE 1830

Pultizer Prize Winning Plays

OUR TOWN
Thornton Wilder

THE PIANO LESSON
August Wilson

THE SHADOW BOX
Michael Christofer

THE SKIN OF OUR TEETH
Thornton Wilder

A SOLDIER'S PLAY
Charles Fuller

STREET SCENE
Elmer Rice

THE SUBJECT WAS ROSES
Frank Gilroy

THEY KNEW WHAT THEY WANTED
Sidney Howard

THE TIME OF YOUR LIFE
William Saroyan

GREAT PLAYWRIGHTS, GREAT PLAYS

James Goldman	THE LION IN WINTER
Robert Bolt	A MAN FOR ALL SEASONS
Neil Simon	PROPOSALS
Alan Ayckbourn	COMMUNICATING DOORS
Samuel Beckett	ENDGAME
Bertolt Brecht	MOTHER COURAGE AND HER CHILDREN
Agatha Christie	THE MOUSETRAP
Noel Coward	BLITHE SPIRIT
Georges Feydeau	A FLEA IN HER EAR
Eugene Ionesco	THE BALD SOPRANO
David Mamet	THE OLD NEIGHBORHOOD
Christopher Hampton	LES LIAISONS DANGEREUSES
Dario Fo	WE WON'T PAY! WE WON'T PAY!
Athol Fugard	VALLEY SONG
George Bernard Shaw	MISALLIANCE
Thornton Wilder	OUR TOWN

These are among the thousands of plays in Samuel French's
BASIC CATALOG OF PLAYS AND MUSICALS

Samuel French, Inc.
THE HOUSE OF PLAYS SINCE 1830